A LAKE HARMONY NOVEL
TANJA WALTRIP

I

Contents

Author Note

I've wanted to write this book for over five years, and I'm so happy I can finally share this town and all its many charming characters. This debut book and new series is full of love, humor, and heat and it introduces a new town and characters that reside about 40 miles west of Chicago. My goal was to create a contemporary romance with seasoned romance and conflicts that could be relatable. I leave a little piece of myself in each character and Lake Harmony is a bit of the Midwest where I grew up with an addition of a lake because who doesn't love water to enjoy in the heat of summer! Julia and Jackson's love story is one many married couples can relate to and I hope you get your happily ever after too!

Acknowledgments

Many people-whether they know it or not-enabled me to write this book. Thank you for your continuous support and "just write it" attitude. Without the love, guidance, and encouragement from all of you, this town and its many characters would still be taking up space in my daily thoughts.

A big shout out to my Starfish Tribe for giving me immediate feedback, a lot of thumbs-up emojis, and guiding me in the right direction. Anna Herring for helping me create my website and for all the technical support. Marnie Sloan for her humor, love, and editing support which made my writing immeasurably better (even if she hated Jackson in the beginning), and I told her that it was expected to which I got "Oh, then well done." Linda Miller, my alpha reader, for reading and believing from the very beginning.

To Emily, for making me a mom and giving me a reason to push myself to be a strong independent role model for you. Remember anything is possible if you just try. I love you.

Dedication

This book is dedicated to all the amazing women in my life and the Julia's out there trying to keep it together.

Thank you for your love, laughter, and all the balls you juggle daily and do it well. Always remember to take your "Me Time" and never feel guilty for it. I've got your back!

Happy Reading ~

Tanja

Chapter One

Julia

I'm sitting on my porch swing, looking into my beautiful home. I live in a gorgeous Craftsman-style home with large open rooms with big windows that span the back of the house, allowing natural light to filter through the windows. I can see my lovely backyard from this spot too. It's the reason I love to sit here. I spend a lot of my time working in my flower gardens and keeping the roses trimmed and blooming. I love living here in Harmony Shores, on Lake Harmony. This is one of those quaint little towns, about 50 miles west of Chicago, where everyone knows everyone. There is a beautiful lake where we can go boating, swimming, and fishing. A happy little hometown where teenagers can't wait to grow up and leave, only to come back home as adults to raise their families in a safe place.

I grew up here, and so did my husband, Jackson. I am from the east side of the lake called Harmony Shores, which has a cute little town square surrounded by charming shops and professional businesses. It's mostly middle-class families working hard to provide the best for their families.

Jackson grew up in Harmony Estates on the north end of the lake. Most of the town residents consider it the more affluent section of town—old money, as many people say. His mom comes from the most affluent family in the town, and they own the Golf Club and Resort on the north end of the lake. They have a huge mansion that sits on the outskirts of town on a couple of acres. I always thought it must have been lonely to be an only child off and away in this huge mansion with no one to play with as a child. I can't even imagine it since I have two brothers and two sisters.

Exhaling, I take another deep breath as I prepare for my family's arrival. *Time to put on the Perfect Julia mask they have all come to expect. Always perfect. Perfect Julia...perfect mom, wife, home, and family. If only life were so damn perfect.*

I'm expecting my parents and siblings for dinner so we can go over the final plans for Mom and Dad's 45th wedding anniversary party that I organized for tomorrow. I hear the doorbell ring-*here we go*. I open the door to Mom and Dad standing there, waiting to come in with big smiles across their faces.

"Mom, Dad, you know you can just walk in. We ARE family, ya know."

"Julia, dear, I know you always tell Dad and me just to walk inn, but this is your home, and we respect you enough to not just barge in. I brought you something, but you better hide it before your brothers show up, or you won't get any of my lemon bars," she says with a wink.

"Come on in; I set us up on the porch."

I quickly go to the kitchen to hide the lemon bars that I love while my parents walk back to the porch. I grab a glass of wine for Mom and me and reach into the fridge for a cold beer for Dad.

Okay, Julia, put on that smile and fake it til ya make it tonight.

Now that everyone is here and has a drink in hand, I bring out the lasagna and salad to the porch with the help of my sisters. Being a large family, we are used to sharing a family-style dinner. The food is always placed in the middle of the table, and the dishes or plates are passed around until everyone has their share.

Dad stands up and says, "Before you all start shoveling your sister's delicious lasagna down, I wanted to take a second just to tell you how proud of you Mom and I are. We couldn't have asked for better kids, and we love you all so very much. Thank you for putting this party together and showing your mom and me a great night surrounded by family and friends for our 45th Anniversary."

I look around the table at my family. You know when you see a large family, and you know just by looking at them, they are related. That is how we look to strangers. The Stone family —the men all have dark hair, sapphire blue eyes and stand over six-foot tall with broad shoulders. The women, except for Stella, all have blonde hair and gray eyes. Stella, our youngest "oopsie," looks just like Dad—dark hair, tall and willowy, with dark blue eyes that look like a stormy night sky.

"Ruby, do you have anything else you want to add or say to the kids while we have their attention, Dear?"

"Yes. I want to remind everyone that the cook doesn't clean after you enjoy this delicious food. Now eat what Julia has so graciously prepared and, boys, leave enough for Jackson."

Garrett, my oldest brother, looks over. "Jules, where is Jackson? Was hoping he'd be here. I haven't seen him in ages."

"He's sorry he missed dinner and family time around the final planning for tomorrow's party, but he said he'd see you all tomorrow. He had to run to the hospital for a patient." *He better make it tomorrow, or I am going to kill him.*

Ellen asks," Where are the kiddos? I figured they would be here with us tonight. Must have gotten a better offer than hanging with their old aunts and uncles, huh?"

"Daniel is out with friends. Probably running around town somewhere. You know how it was when you were sixteen. You were never home on the weekends unless you were forced. Josie is at a sleepover with a friend from dance class. I think she said it was movie night, and they were going to do a *Harry Potter* marathon. Hopefully, that means they pass out by midnight because we have the party tomorrow and I don't need a crabby pre-teen with a sleepover hang-over."

The evening goes smoothly, talking about final arrangements for the party tomorrow and what everyone is handling so that Mom and Dad can just show up and enjoy themselves. We all went in together and bought them a special trip they have been talking about but never booked themselves. Mom and Dad excuse themselves, saying they want to have an early night since tomorrow could keep them out later than usual. My siblings, however, don't seem to have a hurry bone in them and show no signs of leaving.

"Now that Mom and Dad are gone, does everyone know what they need to do tomorrow-or any questions?"

Garrett says, "Jules, thank you for putting this together. We all know that when we casually talked about doing something special for them, no one put anything into motion until you brought it up and made a plan. Without you, I think we would all be lost. Rob would just be walking around in a circle with no direction." Garrett takes a pull from his beer while laughing at his little brother.

"What the hell, man, I'm not an idiot. I can walk a straight line and do many other things. I happen to be quite the charmer. Just ask the ladies." Rob replies, wiggling his eyebrows.

"Guys, let's stay focused for a sec, okay?" Ellen says, shaking her head. Always the level-headed one of us. "Julia did most of this party, and we do appreciate it. I don't know how you always manage to make these parties into the glamorous events that they are with everything else on your plate, but we all love you for it."

Stella says softly, "Thanks for covering my portion, guys. I appreciate your understanding that I just don't have the cash to put my share in. Hopefully soon, though. I'm starting a new job."

Garrett leans over with a smirk and says, "Stella, what is it this time? Florist? Baker? Influencer?"

Rolling her eyes, "Garrett, why do you always have to be the big brother and harass me? I am trying. I just haven't found my niche yet. Can't you give a girl a break! Be supportive, not an ass. Since we're done here, I'm going home. I'll see you guys tomorrow."

I watch as Stella gets up, obviously upset, and gets ready to leave. I stand up and walk with her to the door. On the way out, I grab her arm, and we detour to the kitchen. I take a napkin and grab her one of Mom's lemon bars. "Don't let him upset you. You will figure it out. We all love you and want the best for you. Now go, and don't let them see that lemon bar!" She happily accepts and we have a good laugh as we walk to the door.

Giving me a big hug, she says. "Thanks, Jules—I love you, sis."

"Love you too, and you will figure it out. I am always here to listen or if you just want to come and hang out with me."

Ellen and Scott get up next to head home and say goodbye to the guys. As I walk with them to the door, I watch Scott put his hand on Ellen's low back as he escorts her. When they get to the door, she stops and turns and gives him a soft kiss and says, "Love you."

He replies, "Always."

Smiling at them, "You two have a good night. I am glad that you were here. Tomorrow should be a great night." I stand and watch them walk hand in hand to their car. Scott opened the car door for Ellen and then walked around to the other side. I love seeing how in love they are with each other.

I shut the door and took a deep breath. "Two to go," I mutter, shaking my head and laughing to myself. My brothers would sit here all night and drink all my beer if I let them. *Not tonight, boys.*

"Garrett, how are things at the station? Anything new or crazy going on with the town Sheriff?" I ask, hiding my smile behind my hand.

"Oh, you saw Gertie's post, huh?" he says as he wipes his hand down his face with frustration.

Gertie, our resident gossip. She is 75 years old and runs the town Facebook page Harmony Hears. She works alongside her brother, Peter, who owns the 1-Stop General Store in town, where she tends to overhear everything going on in town. She has absolutely no filter, and anything she hears about town or people living here she believes is fair game to post.

"I saw her post, alright! Who was it about, Garrett? Spill."

Rob holds up a hand, "Wait, I must have missed it-hold on, let me pull it up." Grabbing his phone, Garrett and I watch as he pulls up the Town's Facebook page and reads the post.

Lovers Caught Canoodling In The Library Parking Lot

Two individuals were caught canoodling in the parking lot at the library after hours. The sheriff was called by a concerned citizen of Lake Harmony worried about the tomfoolery and assumed it was teenagers messing around by the library. To his surprise...he found ADULTS that should know better. Shame on you. You know who you are!

"Holy shit! That is hilarious. Who was it? Come on, tell us!"

Garrett sighs, looking back and forth between Rob and me, "Why? Do you guys want to fuel this rumor mill debacle? You're killing me. I'm not telling you because I'm not going to be responsible for two marriages having even more issues."

Rob's eyes bug out, "Wait! Does that mean the 'Adults Canoodling' were not married to each other?"

"No, they are not, and that is the end of it. Both of you, move on."

I laughed along with Rob and watched the horror on Garrett's face as he must be recalling what he interrupted. Okay, time to get these guys out so I can relax before Daniel and Jackson come home.

"Guys, it's a Friday night, so thanks for giving up your social lives to come hash out the last few details for Mom and Dad's party tomorrow, but don't you both usually go to Cooper's Corner on Fridays?" I sit innocently and patiently wait for them to get the hint or realize they have somewhere better to be.

Rob stands up, "Garrett, Jules is kicking us out. She must want alone time. Let's head to Coop's and see who's there. Come on. Be a good wingman, big brother!"

"Fine, I wanted to catch Coop this weekend anyway. May as well do it with a beer at the bar. Let's go and let Jules relax."

After bear hugs and *I love yous*, the guy's head out, and I get to enjoy some peace and quiet. I walk to the kitchen, pour myself a glass of wine, dim the porch lights and sit on my porch swing with my kindle. I've learned that when you wear a lot of hats and tend to be the one that everyone needs something from, the little moments I get to be alone, I cherish. I might as well enjoy it now and wait until Daniel makes it home. I know better than to wait up for Jackson.

Jackson

Thank god today is Friday. It has been a week of one emergency after another, and that is after a full schedule of patients. I feel like I haven't seen my wife and kids or spent much time with them this summer. Not to mention poker night with the guys. I need to stop complaining. I'm helping my patients and providing for my family, and that's what matters.

"Jackson, I know you wanted to try to get out of the office on time today, but Mrs. Porter just walked in with little Joey. She refused to go to the Emergency Room, so she is in exam room two waiting for you. I peeked at Joey's arm, and I don't know that he needs an X-ray, but he does need stitches. You know how Mama Bear is with her Joey, and you are the only doctor that woman trusts."

"I've got it, Paige. Can you stay until I figure out if this is an office visit or if I have to head to the Emergency Room with them?"

"Sure. Let me finish cleaning up the other exam rooms and prepping for Monday. If I do it now, I can come in a few minutes later next week. Come find me when you know the plan for Joey."

Entering the exam room with Mrs. Porter and six-year-old Joey, I ask, "So buddy, what adventures have you been on now to bring you and your mom into my office?"

"Oh, Dr. Harte, thank you for staying at the office so you could see Joey. You know you are the only doctor that we can see. You just know how to handle my little Joey, so he's not scared."

Exhausted but smiling at her, "Well, let's see what we have. Nurse Paige said you hurt your arm. Let's look and see how we can make it feel better."

One look, and I know I better just head to the Emergency Room and ask for an X-ray. If I don't, I know we'll just be back again tomorrow to do it. He'll need stitches.

"First things first, we better clean this up. Joey, I'm going to wash this cut up, and then we need to stitch it up to make it better. I'll ask Nurse Paige to come in with some magic potion first, okay?"

Little Joey has the cutest big eyes and dimples. He slowly shakes his head up and down and says, "Okay."
I step into the hall and see Paige walk out of the exam room next door. "Can you get me the numbing cream and everything I need for sutures, and then it looks like a trip for X-rays."

"Sure thing, give me a second."

Paige comes back in with what I need and looks at Joey. "I have a magic sucker for you. Magic makes you brave. Do you think you can use your own magic while Dr. Jackson helps clean up your arm?" Joey looks at her again and says, "I like magic."

While I start cleaning the area and preparing it for stitches, Paige stays and talks with Joey and his mom to keep them both distracted and not focused on what I am doing. Once I have the stitches finished and a bandage over them to keep them clean, I need to escort them over to the hospital.

"All done, Joey. You were a very brave boy."

"Must have been the magic sucker he got from Nurse

Paige," Mrs. Porter says.

"I would like an X-ray of that arm done, Mrs. Porter. Better safe than sorry. It's swelling quite a bit, and the bruising is starting to really show. Did you give him anything for the pain before coming in?"

"I gave him some Tylenol because he wouldn't stop crying. That was about an hour ago."

"Okay then, let's try to keep that arm still and head over and find out if we need to cast it."

Heading out of the office tell Paige to go ahead and wrap up and head home to her husband. She has been such a great addition to my practice. One of the best things I did was hire her when I opened my practice. She is a long-time resident of Lake Harmony and her years of experience has been a true asset to me starting a new practice and having my own caseload of new patients. She has always been the calming factor in any crisis that walks into our practice. Once again, her knowledge and understanding from experience was a great help with Joey and his mother tonight.

After X-rays and staying with Joey until the orthopedic doctor-on-call could wrap the fractured wrist, I am finally pulling into the driveway. No extra cars, so the family must all be gone. It's ten o'clock, and I am hungry and tired.

Walking into the house, it seems awfully quiet. There are a few lights on, but the place is mainly dark. I'm sure Julia is upset that I missed the family being over, but I'll see them tomorrow at the party. I walked towards the kitchen and sure enough, Julia left a dinner plate for me. All I have to do is warm it up. She made lasagna tonight—one of my favorite meals. I'm more than a little surprised her brothers left me a piece.

Sticking my plate in the microwave, I walk to the fridge for a cold beer and see a salad waiting for me. I smile, knowing that my wife takes good care of me. *Hmm, where is my wife?* I walk towards the porch, and there she is on her porch swing. She loves that thing. I put that up for her for Mother's Day when Daniel was a baby. It's still her favorite spot in the house. She would sit out there with both kids whenever she could.

"Hi, honey, sorry I missed dinner with the folks. Thank you for keeping a plate for me. You know I love your lasagna."

"Hi, what kept you so late tonight?"
I can tell she upset with me, but there wasn't anything I could do about little Joey except give them the full service.

"I had a frantic mother that came in at closing time. We ended up at the hospital for X-rays and a cast. I'm sorry I missed everyone."

"It's fine, Jackson. Was it Mrs. Porter and Joey again?"

I look at her, smiling. "You know she insists I am the only doctor in town that can see him."

Julia looks tired too, and I am sure putting this party together for her parents is making her anxious. She works so hard at keeping everything above water for all of us. When she isn't helping friends or family, she is working in her garden.

She is still just as stunning as when I first fell in love with her. Time has only made her prettier. She keeps her blonde hair long and doesn't wear much make-up. Never has. She has always had that natural beauty with a few sprinkles of freckles on her nose. Her gray eyes always seem to look right through me. Like they are right now.

The microwave dings, and my food is warm. I turn around and walk to the kitchen to grab my dinner and beer, so I can sit on the porch with her.

"Where are the kids?"

"Daniel is out with friends and should be home by curfew. Josie is at a sleepover with her friend."

"I'm glad you have some quiet time then. I know how much you have been balancing lately." She just looks at me, stares quietly, and looks away. She looked like she had something on her mind but didn't want to share it. I wonder what she wanted to say. I am sure she is upset I wasn't here tonight. I finish my dinner and rinse my dishes before putting them in the dishwasher.

"Honey, I'm heading to wash off this long day in the shower. Are you going to be up soon, or do you want me to come back down and sit with you?"

"Go on up. I just want to finish this chapter I'm reading."

"Okay, I'll see you when you come up." I walk over to give her a kiss and then head upstairs to shower and get ready for bed.

Chapter Two

Julia

Twenty minutes! I took twenty minutes to finish my chapter, turn on the dishwasher, lock the doors, and I come upstairs to see my husband sleeping. He is completely out with a soft snore escaping his mouth. I stand there and just look at him. For forty-five, he is still a handsome man. His brunette hair is starting to have more salt and pepper than brown. He's as fit as he was when I married him out of college. He still makes the time to go to the gym. Probably because he needs it to work off the stress from work. God knows he has stress. He is never home because he is always running from one emergency patient to the next when he should be done with office hours. This was not the plan when we talked about him having a family practice here, but the town is growing, and people need a doctor to see close to home. I love him, but he is stretching himself thin. Trying to be the perfect doctor. I just wish he tried being the perfect husband and dad. Somewhere along the way, we have lost our way and priorities have gotten misplaced.

I go to the bathroom and get ready for bed. Wash my face and do my nighttime skincare routine. At forty-four, I'm beginning to see signs of aging on my face, and that is just not acceptable. Plus, no one wants to look at my old hag face tomorrow at the party. Thank god makeup will hide the dark circles under my eyes.

Turning off the light, I change into my pajamas and slowly crawl into bed. I know he is tired and his passing out so quickly only proves that. The last thing I want to do is wake him up.

"Come here," I hear as Jackson pulls me into his chest and wraps his arms around me. I take a deep exhale. If only these moments outnumbered the ones where I feel so lonely.

"I love you, Jules, and I'm really sorry I wasn't here for you tonight."

If only the *sorry's* made up for the constant loss I feel every time he misses something important. I know he is a doctor, and I understand his responsibilities to his patients, but he has a duty to his kids and me, too. When will I be a priority again? At least one of his top two?

"I love you too, Jackson. Let's get some rest because tomorrow is another packed day of running and doing."

I try to clear my mind of the million things floating around in it. Sleep feels a million miles away even though I'm exhausted. After lying in bed wrapped up in Jackson for what seemed like hours, I am still wide awake. At this point, I am not just counting sheep. I have sheep, their goat cousins, Farmer Fred, Sally Scarecrow, and do not even get me started on the damn cows. Good grief, I am going to be hurting tomorrow. I glance at the clock, and it is now two in the morning. I heard Daniel come in quietly at curfew. Thank god he is punctual. If I had two of them never showing up when expected, I'd be living in the nuthouse.

Come on, sleepy time. I promise to go for a long run in the morning. Hey, I will run to Harmonious Bites for my daily caffeine instead of driving. Just let me relax enough to sleep. Pretty please with a cherry on top? Okay, let's try the relaxing technique mom always did with us when we were kids. Start with your toes and relax them into the mattress. Then relax your feet and up into your ankles. Maybe this is working. Keep going, Jules; sleep is around the corner.

Shit! Why am I interrupting the relaxing technique? Back to the ankles and take a deep breath in, deep breath out. Feet and lower legs are getting heavy. Knees, thighs relaxed. My back hurts tonight. I did too much gardening. Good lord, Jules, get back to relaxing, not thinking about your petunias. Back

14

is relaxing, shoulders, jaw, head, and deep breath in and out. Picturing my favorite color is blue. The blue of the lake. Deep breath, in and out.

Chapter Three

Julia

If I slept five hours, I'd be surprised. I feel like a zombie as I lay here staring at my sleeping husband. I have a million things to do for the party, and I need to get my caffeine fix in with the girls this morning at Harmonious Bites. Like I promised the sleep fairy, I will run there today instead of taking the car. I brush the hair away from Jackson's face, smile at my handsome husband, and watch him slowly wake up. He leans forward and kisses the tip of my nose.

"Jackson, I'm going to run over for my coffee with the girls this morning. Can you make sure to be home this morning so that when Josie gets dropped off from her friends at ten, you can decide if our beautiful daughter needs a nap before the party or can help out with picking up her messy room?"

"Absolutely, and good morning honey, when did you finally come to bed last night? I must have dozed off waiting for you. My week caught up to me once I put my head on the pillow."

"Not too long after you came up, but I did not want to wake you. You looked pretty exhausted, so I quietly crawled beside you and went to sleep myself."

"Well, I am going to get up with you. After Josie gets home, I want to get an hour in at the gym if possible before the party, and we start getting ready to leave."

I get up out of bed and head to the bathroom. "Good god!" I do look like a zombie. I need to start taking better care of myself. These dark eyes are a dead giveaway that I am burning the candle at both ends myself.

Jackson yells from the bedroom, "Honey, Gertie posted about your parents on her gossip page. It is a nice post about their anniversary. Make sure you look at it before you leave."

<u>Big Celebration For Our Lovely Stones - 45 Years!</u>
Edison & Ruby Stone (Lake Harmony's High School Sweethearts) will celebrate their 45th anniversary this weekend. Nice to see couples lasting that long, since the norm for these younger couples seems to putter out at about the ten-year mark. Congratulations to you two—show these youngsters how it's done!

Turning the corner into town, I see Harmonious Bites up ahead. I should have sent Ellen a text when I left the house so she would have my coffee ready. Darn it, that's what sisters are for when they own the local coffee house. I walk into the shop, and as the bell above the door chimes, I see Ellen look up with a smile.

"Decided to run in today. I need to wake this body up and let her know there are things to get done and people to see!"

Laughing, "I see that, sis. Usual today or should I spike it with an extra shot of caffeine?"

"YES, PLEASE! Before I fall down. Are the girls in?"

"Yep, they're back at our usual table. Let me grab one of the staff to take over, and I'll join you and bring your coffee back."

"Thanks, love—see you in a few."

Good lord, what is going on! My phone will not stop buzzing. Oh shit, family group text is going. Laughing, I look at the text chain. This should be good.

Rob: Thanks for dinner! I LOVE your lasagna.
Rob: Sorry we overstayed our welcome.
Rob: Saw Hill at Coops with a date *Wink emoji*
Rob: Garrett was an asshole to her again
Rob: His typical buffoon behavior *gorilla emoji*
Stella: He wasn't very nice to his little sister last night either
Garrett: Sorry Stella- I didn't mean to hurt your feelings kiddo
Stella: You are forgiven - this time

Garrett: I WAS NOT AN ASSHOLE TO HILL
Rob: YES, big bro, you were *laugh crying emoji*
Garrett: UGH *Shaking head*
Garrett: Yes, thank you Jules-see you tonight
Ellen: Leave Jules alone, she's having coffee with girls before the chaos

Walking towards the back, where we have our usual table, I see Hillary, Bree, and Sam. My three best friends since we were little. Having grown up together, we're as close as sisters. They're sitting with their coffees and laughing at whatever story Hillary is sharing.

Hillary is the sassiest of the four of us. She owns a catering business in town called *A Matter of Taste* and does most of the high-end parties and gatherings around Lake Harmony. She has dark hair, emerald eyes, and a perpetual smirk on her face...like she's up to no good.

Bree is our sweetheart of the group. Blonde, amber eyes, petite. She teaches Kindergarten at Lake Harmony Elementary School. She refuses to use profanity, so we tend to hear her cursing with such things as *gosh darn donkey biscuits*!

Sam, married to Paul, owns Lansing Design and Gardens in town. She's the Girl Next Door, with natural beauty— wavy brown hair usually pulled up off her face and warm brown eyes. She's our mother hen and tends always to make sure we are all okay and happy. She is the most natural of us and always says it is too much hassle to wear a lot of makeup and work in the dirt. You can usually catch her in her greenhouse attire or with a dirt smear on her cheek.

"Good morning, ladies! What crazy Hillary story am I walking in on?"

Bree says, "Hill was just sharing how her first date went with online Jeff last night."

"Oh, can you please start over? I need some humor in my life this morning if I'm going to get through this day and night."

Ellen comes rushing over to join us at the table with two coffees and a small plate of scones for all of us. Thank god for my sister. I need my caffeine stat!

Hillary smiles, "Oh my god, Jules, it's ridiculous. Now that Ellen has time to join us, too, I'll share with you both. So, I met "online Jeff" about a week ago. On paper, he looked great, they usually do, so I thought *'Okay, Hill, let's do this,'* and you know my rule. I must meet in person within a week or two, or it's see ya later, Charlie. I left it up to him where to meet for our date. Of course, he picks Coop's, but at least I have backup there if it goes south. It was going fine, but he was just not the guy for me. I knew right away that we just didn't click. Then guess who walks in? Garrett and Rob, your annoying brothers. So naturally, they see me and make a beeline for our table. Rob was fine, joking around trying to embarrass me, but Garrett was just a dick. Being rude and his typical arrogant self towards me. That was the final straw, so I ended the date and went home."

Interesting indeed, Hill. She and Garrett act so horrible towards each other, but we all see there is crazy chemistry and hurt feelings underneath all the bickering. We are all just giving it time.

"Sorry they killed your date but maybe it created an easy out for you to ditch the dud?"

Hill laughs, "Eh, whatever. At least I got out of that boring date. If I had to listen to him talk about himself any longer, I was going to climb out the bathroom window. It wouldn't be the first time."

Sam grabs my hand, "So how about you, Jules? You had them all over last night to finalize everything, right? Are you good to go, or do you need anything from us? You know we're always happy to help. I know Hill has the food covered and I'm bringing the red geraniums for the table pieces. Bree is coming early to help put up some of the decorations with the family. Is there anything at all we can do that you don't have covered?"

"I'm all set but thank you for everything you're doing for my parents and this party, guys. The only thing left is to go home, allow a little time to get myself ready, and get the kids loaded up and off to the club."

∞ ∞ ∞

I have about three hours before I need to be ready to leave for the party. I am going to take an hour of 'me' time. Josie is watching a movie after her morning nap on the couch. Thank goodness Jackson got her to lay down on the couch and nap after she came home with her sleepover hangover. He said she was a beast when she came home, and Daniel texted, saying he wanted to flush her head in the toilet. Ah, brotherly love. I know all about that!

A long soak with my book sounds perfect to de-stress before the next round kicks in today. I grab my lavender salts, pour a heavy handful into the bath, and add just a bit of my lavender oil. The kids know I need this time, so hopefully that means they listen and give me my hour. I hear a scratch at the door and open it to find Duke, our Great Pyrenees, who is about two years old.

"Hey, buddy, Mom is going to take a soak, so if you come in here, you have to be a good boy and lay down, k?" He comes what can only be referred to as sashaying in the bathroom, lays down on the rug in front of the tub with a sigh, and closes his eyes. At least this one is typically quiet, except when protecting us from squirrels, leaves, cars, and pretty much anything in motion.

Me-Time is starting. I grab my book and glass of water and slide down into the lavender bath to soak, relax, and get lost in my romance novel. After a few minutes, my eyes are getting too heavy to continue reading, so I put my book down. I lie back and just try to relax, but of course my mind starts thinking back to other times in my life I was relaxing in a lavender bath and primping for important events. Special moments with Jackson like our birthdays and important dates that followed. I always made sure that I felt and looked my best so he would be proud to have me on his arm. It's been a while since we've had a reason to celebrate and get gussied up for an event. I'm looking forward to

21

putting on my new dress and knocking my husband's socks off.

After my bath, I go downstairs to see Josie still watching a movie and snuggling with the dog, who apparently left me and found a better snuggle buddy.

"Hey, sweetie, do you want to shower before we head out to Gram and Gramp's party in a bit? We have to leave the house in about an hour or so."

"Mom, if I do, will you have time to put a few curls in my hair around my face? I know you still need to get ready, so, if not, that's okay. I just wanted to look extra special for them."

Looking at my twelve-year-old daughter is like looking at myself at that age. She has the same blonde hair and gray eyes. She has a long, graceful figure since she spends every minute in dance classes. The only thing she does not have from me are Jackson's dimples, which I like to tell her are kisses from the angels.

"Of course, honey, I always have time for you. How about you go on up, take a shower, and dry your hair. By the time you're done with that, I can put some curls in your hair. You can put your party dress on after we finish your hair. Do you know where your brother is?"

"He's on the porch on his phone."

I give her a quick kiss, send her on her way upstairs and look for my son. I find Daniel on his cell phone talking to someone about how he is busy with family stuff tonight and will not be able to go out with the guys. Sixteen and never home seems to be the norm with this guy. He hasn't noticed that I'm here yet, so that gives me a moment just to watch him. Dark hair like his dad but with the sapphire blue eyes from the Stone side. He is a cool dude for a teenager, and even if he doesn't want to admit it, I know he adores Josie and will do anything she asks. I can thank Garrett and Rob for that—they set the bar high for being good brothers and good influences for the most part. Daniel looks up, sees me, and says goodbye to whoever is on the other end of the phone.

"Hey, Mom, sorry I didn't see you standing there, or I

would've hung up quicker."

"No worries, Daniel. I just wanted to make sure that you're going to be ready to leave on time. We have about an hour or so before we need to leave for the party. Have you heard from your dad? Did he happen to call the house while I was in the bath?"

"No, I haven't heard from him since he left this morning. I'm going to go head up, but do I have to wear a suit and tie? You know, Uncle Rob never wears a tie with his suit."

"You're right. No, you don't have to wear a tie. We should all be as comfortable as possible, but you do need to wear the suit. I want us to look sharp tonight. All of us," I say with a wink, watching as he takes off up the stairs.

I better check my cell phone for any messages. Jackson should have been home by now. I walk over to the kitchen, where my phone is on the counter. Sure enough, he sent me a text. *This better be good.*

Jackson: Honey, got paged to the hospital for baby- meet you @party

I better head up and finish getting ready to get the kids out the door and there on time.

After dressing and helping Josie with her curls, it's time to go. "Kids, Dad is going to meet us at the party since he's at the hospital delivering a baby. Can you both head to the car so we can get there on time, please?"

As I turn to grab my purse, I catch Daniel's expression, and he looks angry. After Josie walks towards the garage I turn to him and ask, "Hey, buddy, you okay?"
"It's nothing, Mom. It'd just be nice if Dad could be with us for once and not at the hospital. He seems to be missing everything lately. But let's go and have a good time with the family. I'm

excited to see Gram and Gramps get their gift we all got for them. Do you think they'll be surprised?"

"I do, Daniel, I do," I say with a big smile.

My parents have always wanted to go to Europe, but with such a big family and Dad running Stone Builders, they just never seemed to have the time. Now that Mom is retired from teaching and Rob is about to take over the newest project at the company, it opens them up to take a trip they've put on the shelf for too long.

Chapter Four

Jackson

Sitting here having my coffee and quick breakfast this morning, I can't stop thinking about Jules and that look she gave me last night. Like she had something serious on her mind but did not want to voice it. I know she is exhausted and always the go-to person for everyone, but she usually enjoys all the organizing. I will have to try to plan a night out for the two of us soon. I cannot remember the last time we did something alone as a couple.

I let the family know I'm heading out for an hour at the gym. I like to get time when I can, so I don't get the dreaded "dad bod." Running a couple of miles usually gives me time to turn everything floating in my head off for a bit. I always have a lot of pressure on my shoulders with work and my patients, along with making sure my family has what they need.

I am just finishing my warmup on the treadmill and heading to the weights when I see the SOS message from the service that covers the office over the weekends. Please, not another emergency right now.

"Hello, this is Dr. Harte… Okay, I'm on my way."

It never fucking fails. I love my job and my patients, but Jules will kill me if this takes me away from the party later. I better get over to the hospital.

Here I am at the hospital when I should be with my family at a very important celebration for my in-laws. Jules will be pissed again, but babies have their own schedules and can't be put on hold.

"Dr. Harte, Sally is about halfway there."

I wonder how much longer her husband will be upright. The last time I walked in there, he looked rather green and had to sit down. I don't think he is handling the delivery of this first baby too well."

I stand up and grab the chart. I better go calm Dad down, or we're going to have him passing out and in a hospital bed next to her.

Walking into their room, "Sally and Greg, how are you two holding up in here? We're about halfway there before we can start pushing. Greg, you have time if you want to grab some fresh air. I can have someone stay in here with Sally while you're out."

"No, I won't be able to relax if I leave this room. I'll be okay. It's just hard to watch your wife be in so much pain. I wish I could help her more."

"You two went to Lamaze class, right? Let's focus on her breathing. Do you have tennis balls? Do they still teach that?"

"Honey, I totally forgot about that. Let me get the tennis balls, and I can start working on giving you some help. Do you need any more ice chips? I don't want you to dehydrate."

"Alrighty, it looks like you both have a plan in place. Never know how long babies take the first time around, but you're progressing nicely. I'm going to head back to the nurse's station and make sure everything is in place for this little one to arrive. If you need something, just use the nurse call button, and someone will come in. I can watch the monitors from the station."

Pacing back and forth in the delivery room waiting for my first child to be born I keep one eye on Julia and one on the baby monitor watching for any signs of trouble. My nerves are at a no return point and my beautiful wife is calmly handling this baby delivery like a pro. She asks me to sit and take a deep breath. Here she is trying to deliver a baby and once again worried about me. I understand the reasons now why as a doctor you should never treat someone you care about. I go sit down next to her and hold her hand, ask if she needs any more ice chips, but she just smiles and tells me to please relax, everything will be fine.

The delivery took almost 15 hours and through it all she continued to push when directed and catch her breath between contractions. Watching my son be born into the world and taking his first breath, all pink and wrinkly, is the most amazing moment I have ever experienced. My son, Daniel, with a head full of dark hair like mine. He is a good-sized baby for Julia at almost 9 pounds. Healthy with all his fingers and toes and strong lungs that continue to bring cries into the room. I will do anything to keep my family happy and safe.

Okay, it is finally go-time to deliver this first baby for Sally and Greg. First babies like to make their own schedule, and their delivery time can either come at warp speed or take the long way here. I sent Julia a text that I'm still at the hospital, so at least she knows I will not make the party. It sucks that I would not see everyone and celebrate, but this is my job and what I signed up for.

"Are you ready to have a baby, Sally?" I say as I walk into the delivery room, where they anxiously wait for the baby's arrival.

"Sally and Greg, you have a beautiful and healthy baby boy. I remember when my son, Daniel, was born. It goes so fast, so enjoy every moment you have with him. He is a cute little guy."

As I walk to the nurse's stations to grab my things and finally head home, I stop and take a deep breath. Smiling, I remember holding both of my kids that first time. There's nothing better than seeing a child born, especially one you had a part in bringing into this world. That moment—when you hold your baby in your arms for the first time—it's like no other.

"Dr. Harte, you sure are at the hospital a lot these days. You must work more than you're at home," the delivery nurse says to me.

"It sure feels like that some days, but my patients need me and there is nothing better than a healthy baby delivery."

It has been another long day for me, and I know walking in at two in the morning isn't going to win me any points with my wife. Hopefully, she'll understand that this is my life. I am a doctor and on-call to handle patients. It should not be a huge surprise. As I go up to bed, I quietly walk through the dark bedroom into the master bath, trying to avoid waking my wife. I just stand there in the shower letting the hot water run over me. I could sleep for a week.

As I walk out of the bath and towards our bed, I realize there is no Julia in bed sleeping. Where the hell is she? I know she is home because I saw the car in the garage.

I grab some boxers to throw on and go quietly through the hall to see if she is with Josie. As I slowly open the door to Josie's bedroom, I see Duke in front of the bed, so she must be in here. He never leaves her side. "Shh, Duke, it's okay. Go back to sleep." Sure enough, Julia is snuggled up with Josie, and they are both sound asleep. I'm not going to wake her because I know she is just as exhausted. My two beautiful girls are sleeping in front of me. Looking at Josie reminds me so much of a younger version of my wife. She is her mini-me for sure. I may as well go to bed and talk to her in the morning.

Chapter Five

Julia

The kids and I arrive at the club where the party is being held. I park and head to the party room with the kids. We took the big room with two French doors open to a stone patio area with tables. That way, people can flow from inside to outside if they wish to enjoy the evening. The minute I walk into the room, I see my siblings helping Sam put the flower arrangements around the room and Hillary setting up the food buffet with Griffin, her catering assistant. Bree's already adding twinkle lights to the potted trees Sam brought in from the greenhouse. Everything looks amazing, and Mom and Dad are going to love it.

Hillary spots me and starts to head over. "Jules, I have the cake you ordered in the kitchen here. I want to keep the buttercream refrigerated until we are about to serve it. I made chocolate with raspberries and it looks...well, wait 'til you see it. I amaze myself sometimes. I even added a few fresh flowers on the top tier."

"You are amazing, Hill, and thank you so much for making it special for my parents. The room looks fantastic!"

***

The guests have arrived, mingling, and looking around the room with smiles. The party was the perfect night I wanted for Mom and Dad. A room full of their friends and family and delicious food and dessert. As I walk around the room, I get compliments from everyone on how I (once again) organized the perfect party. Of course, I love the compliments, but a part of me still feels empty. And. unfortunately, many are asking me where my husband is, to which I reply he is at the hospital doing his doctor duties.

Where the hell is Jackson! I mutter under my breath. Another day, another party missed. I should be used to this by now, but that does not mean it is okay. He should be here. Even his parents are here.

I walk over to the area where my siblings are and sit down. Mom and Dad follow me over and ask if they can have a moment to speak to all the guests at the party.

Rob says, "Of course! This is your party, so you can do whatever you want!"

Then he stands up, sticks his fingers in his mouth, and whistles to the guests. Dad looks over at him like he wants to smack him in the back of the head for acting like a fool while mom just smiles and rolls her eyes like *what do you expect?* This is Rob and his typical behavior.

"Excuse my son, everyone, but he did get your attention," Dad says as he grabs Mom's hand.

"Ruby and I are so happy you are all here celebrating our 45th anniversary. Seems like just yesterday I asked this beautiful woman to marry me, and here we are 45 years later with five grown kids and 2 grandkids. Life has a way of throwing you some bumps in the road, but with a great partner, you learn how to go over or around depending on the bump. I hope that all my children have a partner like I do with my wife. Ruby, do you want to add anything, Dear?"

"As Edison said, we're so happy you are all here with us. I would like to thank my children for putting this lovely evening together. We all know that the organizing was Julia's doing, and she did a remarkable job filling this room with lots of love and memories. Please enjoy Miss Hillary's delicious food and cake—it's too good to pass up! Thank you again from both of us."

Mom and Dad then walk over to me and embrace me with hugs.

"Where is Jackson?" they both ask.

"He got called to the hospital earlier and said he would meet us here. I hope he still makes it before too long."

With a concerned look, Mom grabs me by the waist and pulls me towards the patio doors. There aren't too many people outside since we just talked about the food Hill brought and how they should try it.

"Honey, I don't want to upset you, but you look exhausted. Was this party too much to throw on your already busy plate?"

"Absolutely not, Mom. I wanted to do this for the both of you. I am a little tired. I didn't get much sleep last night, but I'm okay."

"Well, I just worry about you, and I know you are upset that he's not here with you and with all of us. I guess that's the life of a doctor though."

Great, now I cannot even put my *Perfect Julia* mask on right. Mom saw right through me and knows that I'm upset, and something is wrong. Where the hell is my husband! This is getting ridiculous. I'm tired of not being able to count on him. Mom and I walk back into the room, and I watch Dad grab her hand and pull her onto the dance floor.

I stood there looking around the room at everyone that came to celebrate. Rob is hitting on one of the pretty bartenders, which is to be expected. Garrett is standing watch over the room as the ever-ready Sheriff. Ellen and Scott are talking with Sam and Paul at the table and laughing. Hill is with Griffin, her sidekick at work and Stella's best friend. They're replenishing the food and slicing more cake. Stella is on the dance floor with Josie dancing like a wild bohemian and singing along with the music. Daniel is filling his plate for probably the third time. My family is happy. Me, not so much.

Walking up to me with a smile is my favorite lady, Miss Jane. She always has such a calming tone and energy.

"Hey, sweetie, this is a beautiful party you created for your parents. They seem to be having a wonderful time, as do all the guests. How come you seem a bit sad?"

Jane, my mother's best friend, and the second mom in my

31

life, patiently stands there looking at me with concern in her eyes. I cannot talk about this. Not here. Not this moment because if I do, I will lose it.

"Jane, I'm alright, just a bit tired. I need to grab my brothers and sisters because we have one more surprise in store for Mom and Dad tonight."

Walking over to the table where my siblings and I have our gift, I gesture to them to come on over.

"Let's go ahead and give them their present. Many are still enjoying food and cake, and soon the older crowd will want to head out."

I walk over to Daniel and Josie, who are at a nearby table, and ask them to please come up with us to give Gram and Gramps their surprise. Josie is beaming, she is so excited to see their reaction, and Daniel is quiet and not saying much.

I lean into him and ask," Daniel, is everything okay? You seem off tonight?"

"Where's Dad? He promised he would be here, and yet again, he is MIA."

"I know, honey, he is stuck delivering a baby, but he said he would meet us here."

We get the attention of the guests again thanks to the ear-piercing whistle by Rob and give my parents their trip to Europe. Both are completely surprised and speechless. They give us all big hugs, and the guests all clap and talk about how lucky they are to have such an incredible family and what an amazing gift.

My phone in my purse vibrates. Please be Jackson saying he is finally on his way.

Jackson: Stuck @ work-baby delivery just starting

Standing there staring at my phone, I can feel my blood pressure rise. Tears sting the backs of my eyes, threatening to spill over, and I better get it together fast because I'm in a room with everyone my family knows. Everyone and their mother are at this party; my husband is MIA. Trying to keep the tears from falling, I walk out of the room and head toward the bathroom. Thankfully, when I enter, I am alone and go to the last stall. Before I even get the door shut, the tears are falling.

Why am I not important to my husband? What must happen to make me a priority or our family a priority? How many more memorable moments do I have to celebrate alone without him? I am so tired of doing this alone and not having him in my life. I just cannot do this anymore. I am not happy. I make sure everyone else is happy and living their best life, and I am completely fucking miserable. What the hell do I need to do to make myself important to him? Something needs to change. We can't keep going on like this. I'm taking charge of my life and putting myself first for once, dammit. I'm sick and tired of being taken for granted or forgotten.

I grab some tissue and clean up my face before leaving the stall. Walking to the mirror, I pull some makeup out of my purse and fix my raccoon eyes the best I can. As I apply lip gloss, I see Gertie enter through the reflection in the mirror.

"Oh, hello, darling," she says as her eyes narrow at me.

I am praying that she cannot tell I just had a major breakdown in the bathroom stall. Here we go—*fake it til ya make it, Julia.*

"Hello, Gertie," I say, proceeding with caution. "I hope you're having a great time. We're so happy for my mom and dad and had such a great turnout for the party!"

"Yes, it has been lovely. You did another spectacular job. Are you okay, dear? You look a bit upset?"

"Oh, I am a bit tired. You know me, wanting to make sure everything was perfect. I better get back to the party and make sure everyone is eating the food. It's too good to waste."

Good grief, she is the last person I needed to run into at that moment. Gossip Gertie! I need a drink, and then I'm going to attempt to enjoy myself since I know Jackson is not going to show. I can damn well enjoy this party alone.

I head to the open bar and ask for a glass of wine. As I wait for the bartender, I see Gertie rush back over to the table of the Widow's Crew. I watch her as she enthusiastically talks to the ladies. All at once, she points at me, and they all turn to look. *Awesome. Fucking awesome. Well, not too subtle, Gertie.*

Smiling at them, I look away, trying to find my next move. I grab my glass of wine and see Garrett sitting at a table alone, so I walk over to join him.

"Hey, Jules, you did an amazing job with this party. Everyone says it was a group effort, but they all know this was all you."

"Thanks, Garrett. It sure turned out lovely, didn't it?

"Sure did, so...where is Jackson, or should I not ask?"

Slowly, I turn and look at my big brother's eyes and see his concern. Shit, I just cannot do this tonight.

"Garrett, I love you, but I can't tonight. I just can't."

Seeing the tears start to form in my eyes, he puts his hand on mine and squeezes. He knows. He is my brother, my biggest protector, and he knows not to say another word right now.

Nope, I'm not enjoying myself, and since the party is handled and coming to an end, I need to get out of here. I need time to myself. I need to think, and I cannot do it here in a room full of people watching. Let me find the kids and get them ready to head home but first, where are the girls?

I walk over to the table where my best friends are sitting, and as I approach, I watch as their eyes study me. All three have their eyes glued to me, and as I get closer, I see the concern on their faces increase. They can probably tell I had a major breakdown in the bathroom, and my eyes are probably a mess—nothing I can do but get the hell out of here as soon as possible.

"Hey, coffee tomorrow, 9:30?"

I see them all start to want to ask me questions, but if they start, I'm going to lose my shit here in this room right now, and I still need to say goodbye to my mom and dad and get the kids home. So, with a deep breath, I look at my friends, shake my head, and just put my hand up to stop them from asking any questions.

"Not now, I can't. I'm barely holding my shit together."

They all nod okay and smile. This is what best friends are all about. They know when to ask, push, support, laugh, or cry. They are my tribe of woman warriors. Thank god I have them in my life, but it's time to escape this party.

∞∞∞

I am completely exhausted and ready to collapse. As the kids and I walk into the house, Josie grabs my hand, and Daniel walks quickly upstairs, saying goodnight over his shoulder. If possible, steam would be coming out of his ears.

Josie stops and looks up at me, "Hey, Mom, can you come snuggle with me tonight. We can talk about how happy Gram and Gramps were at their party. It was a really nice party, Mom."

I squeeze her hand and tell her to head on up. "I'm going to come up in a second and get ready for bed, too, but I would love to come snuggle and talk about the party with you. Go on up and get ready for bed. I'll be there in a second after I check on Duke Dog." She gives me her sweet smile and heads upstairs.

Letting the dog out into the yard one more time, I take the time to just breathe. "Come on, Duke, let's go to bed. You can join me in Josie's bed."

Chapter Six

Julia

I wake up early and quietly leave Josie's room with Duke. "Come on, boy, let's go out." I walk downstairs quietly and let Duke out in the yard. I slept a little bit last night, but I want to get out of here before Jackson comes down. I cannot deal with his millionth *sorry I missed the party* crap this morning. Who knows when he arrived home last night, or should I say this morning? I walk up to the bedroom, and there he is, sound asleep.

Quietly, I grab some running clothes. I need to run this angry energy out of me before I start to lose it, and I'm meeting the girls at Harmonious Bites in a little bit. I have just enough time to get dressed, feed the dog, and leave a quick note. The kids can sleep in and manage their own breakfast with their dad.

As I jog over to Harmonious Bites to meet the girls, I have time to think and sort my emotions and thoughts. Last night was quite overwhelming for me, throwing my parents a beautiful party celebrating their love and being married for 45 years. That is a rarity these days, as most people realize, and a big fucking smack across my face at how my marriage compares. At this rate, I don't think Jackson and I will even hit our next anniversary.

Here we go. I take a deep breath as I get to the shop door and open it. As the bell chimes over the door, I see my best friends sitting at our usual table with worried looks and Ellen behind the counter. I walk over to my sister. "Good morning! Can I have my usual with an extra shot?" She nods yes and lifts her eyebrow at me. "Are you okay, sis? I know you're here to talk to us, but before we join the girls, seriously—are YOU okay?"

I stand looking at my sister and take a deep breath. "No. Ellen, but I sure as hell will be! I'll wait for you to join us before I say anything. Love you."

"Love you too, Jules. I will be right there."

I walk over to the girls and sit down. Here we go, time to drop the bomb and open the next door to finding myself and my happiness. "Good morning, ladies. Thank you for meeting me. Before you all start rambling off questions and voicing concerns, I want to wait for my sister to join us, okay?" They all just smile and nod at me, although I can tell there is concern in their reactions because they know me and can tell something major is about to happen.

Ellen comes over to the table and sits down, and all at once, they slowly turn and look at me, waiting for me to say something. Well, there's no time like the present to make my announcement. "I'm going to ask Jackson for a separation."

Crickets! Shock? No reaction for a minute until, one by one, they realize I'm serious, and then all have bug eyes and gasp simultaneously. Still staring at me until slowly, their expressions change from shock to worry. Ellen grabs my hand and squeezes. "Jules, I think I can speak for all of us that your happiness comes first, but are you sure? Are you sure this isn't a little drastic? Why don't you take the time to talk it out, okay?"

"I am so unhappy, you guys. I'm married and yet completely miserable and lonely. I don't have a good marriage anymore, and I feel taken for granted and forgotten by my husband. I just thought maybe if I wasn't always there waiting for him, he would notice and start to make me a priority again. Right now, I might as well be his housekeeper who has sex every Saturday, and that is only when he is fucking home!"

"What the fuck Jules? When did things get so bad?" Hill says to me. "Do I need to kick his ass? I will do it, you know. I may be little, but I am mighty, and one swift kick in the bazooka and he will go down. You know I've got your back."

Bree takes a deep breath and mumbles, "Donkey balls and firecrackers!" Our resident non-cursing Kindergarten teacher.

Sam and Ellen, the two who are married in my group of friends, look at each other and then at me. Ellen takes my hand and says, "I think you need to talk to someone. This isn't something where you can make a rash decision. I also think that talking to someone with no bias is the healthiest way to approach this. Let me run to the office and grab something. Just sit here quietly for a second and drink your coffee. Everyone take a minute to drink your damn coffees—no talking! Breathe, Jules; it will be okay. I promise. Things will be okay."

While Ellen gets up to go to her office, I do as suggested and drink my coffee. Even if Ellen hadn't told us to zip it, I think my friends are all still too shocked to say much more to me. We all just look at each other. The glances go around the table. There is a lot of emotion behind the eyes of my three best friends, but no one says a word. I watch as Ellen comes back out of her office with something in her hand. She sits down and puts a business card in front of me.

I pick up the card and look at it. It reads Dr. Rose, Psychologist. I guess I'll hear her out. "Ellen, Dr. Rose?"

"Jules, I want you to make an appointment sooner than later because you obviously have a lot of emotion and frustration rolling around in that pretty head of yours. Call her and make an appointment as soon as you can get in. Don't worry about Josie or needing to be somewhere else. One of us will cover for you, right, girls? ` ` She looks at my best friends, and they all nod.

Sam looks at me and says, "Jules, you need to vent and talk things through. I think Ellen is right and that you should make this appointment. We know you love Jackson and Jackson loves you. Somewhere along the way, priorities have just blurred, and maybe Dr. Rose can help clear the path for you to find some balance and happiness again."

Chapter Seven

Jackson

Poker Night with the guys at Garrett's house is a standing "date" where we all meet on the last Thursday of the month. It's always a great time to catch up with the guys. Our typical group includes:

Julia's brother, Rob, entertains us with talk about his latest dating techniques and conquests

Cooper, Garrett's best friend from the Army and owner of the towns bar and grill, Cooper's Corner

Paul, who's married to Julia's best friend Sam and owns the Landscape Design and Garden center

Scott, who is married to my sister-in-law, Ellen, is Stone Builder's Architect

Garrett, my other brother-in-law, who is the town Sheriff

These fools are participants in our monthly poker night.

As we sit around the poker table, all set with drinks and poker snacks, Garrett says to me, "Wow, Jackson! I haven't seen you for poker night in a long time. Nice of you to allow us to see your ugly mug again."

I didn't want this to come up tonight but seeing as there is some trouble brewing, I better calm the waters. "I've been pulled in too many directions lately. I swear my patients are all against me and throwing emergencies at me left and right. I am their doctor, so I just have to suck it up and go."

Suddenly, Paul and Scott have guilty looks on their faces. I look back and forth at them and ask, "WHAT? You two are sitting there looking guilty about something. What the hell is up?"

Scott takes a deep breath, looks at Paul, and says, "I'm guessing you know what I know because the girls talked, right?" Paul just nods his reply and lifts his shoulders. Scott straightens up and looks back at me, "Ellen told me that Julia met the girls at Harmonious Bites Sunday morning after the party. She told them she was leaving you. I guess we are just wondering if you were going to bring it up?"

Shocked, I looked around the table at my friends, "Did you all know this?"

Garrett and Rob stare at me with pissed expressions on their faces. Garrett finally shouts, "NO! I sure didn't. What the fuck is going on with you two? Every time I see Jules, she looks like she is barely holding it together. She keeps piling more and more obligations onto her plate, most likely so she doesn't have to stop and think about life and what's going on between you two. I want to kick your ass, Jackson! I'm sure this is because you are never around. When was the last time you spent any time with your wife or kids?"

"I know. When Jules told me she was going to leave me, I felt sucker punched. I know I've been working too much, but I was also trying to provide for my family and make sure they had everything that they needed. My patient load has nearly doubled in the last couple of years. I'm exhausted, but I just don't have time to stop and think about how to make things better. My wife is miserable, and, fuck, I barely noticed. Trust me, the last thing I want is to lose my family."

"What's your plan, Jackson? How are you going to fix this?" Garrett says on an exhale.

"I'm not sure yet, but at least Jules is willing to work with me instead of just throwing me out of her life. I will fix this; I promise you guys. Can we just have our poker night? I need to have a guys' night and not think about the rest for a couple of hours."

42

The guys look sympathetic and nod at me. At least they're giving me the night to unwind.

It only takes a few minutes, but things start to feel more normal. Rob shares his latest date story about how he met Suzie while on the lake with his boat. They went out last weekend, and she was more handsy than he wanted. He had us all laughing, talking about how she managed to get thrown off the tube and lost her bikini top and wouldn't get out of the water until she got a t-shirt to put on in the water. He gave her a white one. Of course!

Chapter Eight

Jackson

As we walk up to the front door at my in-laws for the traditional Sunday family dinner, I notice Julia is as far away from me as she can be. She hasn't spoken to me much this week, always busy doing one thing or another. I am giving her the space she's so bluntly showing me she needs. Josie is carrying dessert that she made this morning. I think it is cupcakes, her double chocolate with sprinkles, that she loves to eat.

We walk into the house, the last of the group to arrive, and Ruby gives me a big hug. Edison squeezes my shoulder and asks if I want a beer but looking around the room at everyone else. I feel like I walked into my funeral. The guys are just staring at me, unsure what to say to me, and Ellen is being pleasant but very quiet. The only person acting semi-normal is Stella, who walks over to me, smacks me in the arm, and says, "Hey, stranger!" and flits away. Fuck, this is going to be brutal, and I know I'm going to walk away from this dinner with indigestion like a volcano in my gut.

Ruby turns to Jules and the kids and pulls them into the family room as Edison looks at me. "Come help me get some drinks in the kitchen."

"Sure. Happy to help." I follow him into the kitchen and watch as he moves to the fridge to grab me a beer and Jules a glass of wine.

"How are things going at work, Jackson? You seem to have quite the patient load these days, huh?"

So, this is how the confrontation is going to start. "Yeah, I have a rather large patient load, and it takes a lot of my time. The town is growing and bringing more people into the area. Shoot, you should know, considering Stone Builders is putting up one of the newest subdivisions right now. That brings in many young families who all need and want a local doctor. They don't want to drive too far, especially since the hospital is on the other side of the lake. Many of them just go to urgent care because they can't get into my schedule. It makes me feel like I'm not doing enough, but there aren't more hours in the day."

"I hear you, son, the town is growing, and even though it is good for business for both of us, I do understand how it affects your office hours. Is there anything you can do to lift some of the burden off your shoulders?"

"There are a couple of things I can do; I just haven't had the time to put anything in motion yet."

"We were sorry that you missed the party last week. Julia did a great job again. Ruby and I had a wonderful night."

I love my father-in-law, but I know where he is going with this and I feel the guilt being piled on me.

"Ruby and I are worried about all of you. Julia is so busy with all her commitments that she is slowly working herself to the point of burnout. You spend so much time with patients that you miss everything at home. I will stay out of it a little longer, but I'm starting to see its effects on our grandkids. That is where I am having trouble staying out of it."

"I know, Edison, and like I told your sons, I am making this a priority to fix and soon. My family is the most important thing in the world to me, and I will do whatever I have to not to lose them."

He smiles, taps me on the shoulder, and says, "I know, Son. I just wanted to make sure you were on top of it. Ruby and I are going to postpone our trip for a little longer. I need to get this new section of the build plotted and handed over to Rob before we can leave, and I can relax about work. We sure are looking forward to getting away, though."

I watch as Ruby and Jules walk back into the kitchen. My

wife walks over to me and whispers in my ear. "You okay?" I just smile and give her a kiss with a wink, letting her know all is good.

Ruby walks over to Edison, "Stop monopolizing Jackson's ear. We need to get the roast out of the oven."

Edison grabs her and kisses her. "I love you more today than 45 years ago, Ruby."

Looking into Jules's eyes, I see they are watery, so I kiss her and put my arm around her.

Stella comes into the kitchen since she still lives at home in the garage apartment. "Okay, everyone, stop with the lovey-dovey stuff. Mom, what can I help you with?"

Ruby smiles at her youngest and says," Why don't you whip up the salad and slice the fresh bread. I made a roast and some sides that are about ready to come out of the oven. Cut a lot of bread so we can fill up your brothers with bread, not the entire roast." They all laugh, as my brother-in-law's appetites are a long-running joke in the family.

The rest of the family dinner seems to go as normal as possible. Everyone is talking about the party, which makes me feel guilty, but, from the sounds of it, the party was a huge success. Edison and Ruby share with the rest of the family what he told me in the kitchen, that they will hold off on taking that trip until he can hand over the new building site to Rob and not have as much still in the process of closing out.

We have a nice night with the family—it's not often that we can all get together. With such a large family, one or two of us typically have other obligations, usually me. After dinner and dessert, everyone gets ready to head home. It's Sunday night, and we all have work in the morning.

As we walk out, Garrett catches my eye, so I walk over to him again and see Rob join us.

"Jackson, I'm glad you made it tonight. It was good to see your family here with you. I know you can't help medical emergencies that pull you away, just like I can't help if an emergency pulls me into Sheriff mode. I just wanted you to know that if you need Rob or me, we're here for you, Jules, and the kids. Don't think that you don't have our support, okay?"

Rob says, "I know that I am the goofball of the family, but I can put on my big boy pants and be an adult when I need to be, so ditto what Garrett said, okay, man?"

"Thanks, guys. I appreciate that a lot. Better get back to my family and get them home. Night."

Chapter Nine

Julia

Today is the day I see Dr. Rose for the first time. I feel like I have barely survived the last ten days. I'm sure Jackson thinks I am mad at him for missing the party. I am, but there is more to my anger than just that. I could list at least ten times in the last couple of months he has let me down one way or another, which is part of what makes me feel like this shell of myself. I am so lonely and feel like I have no self-worth anymore. I know that I can't keep living like this, so let's hope good ole doc has some answers for me.

Dr. Rose's office is in a cute little Victorian house on an off-street. Nice to know I don't have to do this close to town where everyone will see me going into therapy. Not that therapy is embarrassing, but we all know Gertie would make it so. *Okay, Jules, let's do this.*

The office is friendly and inviting with its blue tones. There is a well-worn tan leather sofa with soft pillows, many green plants, and a peaceful picture of a meadow. Dr. Rose sure knows how to set the mood. There is only one door, which I assume is her office. Five minutes after I sit down, the door opens, and a lovely older woman with round-rimmed glasses and bright green eyes walks toward me. "Hello, I'm Dr. Rose, and you must be Julia Harte."

"Nice to meet you, Dr. Rose; you came highly recommended by my sister, Ellen Whitfield."

She shakes my hand and extends her hand to welcome me into her office. I walk ahead, and she follows me in and sits down across from me. "I'm happy to meet you today, Julia. When we briefly talked about making the appointment, you mentioned your marriage. So how about you just talk a little bit about yourself and what brings you in here today? We can move on from there. Does that sound alright to you?" I nod and smile.

After what seems like a grueling hour of talking about myself, my hopes, fears, and feelings, I am completely exhausted, but I also have a plan. Since I can't go straight home with all this information and thoughts in my head, I head to Harmonious Bites to see my sister. Let me give her a quick text that I'm coming in.

Julia: Finished @ you-know-who and coming 4 coffee
Ellen: C U in a few-love U

Even though I feel a little exhausted from the last hour being on an emotional roller coaster, I have a plan, and no one puts a plan in motion better than I do. I park my car and walk into Harmonious Bites. Ellen is behind the counter, but when she sees me, she steps out, walks directly up to me, and gives me a huge hug. "Wow, that was quite the welcome. How come I don't get a bear hug every time I walk into your shop?"

Smiling and holding my hand, "Well, today is a special day, and I wanted to show you that I love and support you. Can I get you a coffee, tea, water, maybe a brownie?"

"I will take my usual, thanks. Even though I have not been sleeping well, I still need to get a caffeine jolt to get through talking about what just transpired." Ellen walks around the counter to start my coffee when I hear the bell chime above the door and turn to see my three best friends rushing inside. "What in the world are you three up to?"

"GIRL POWER! Ellen texted us letting us know you would be here, and you may need us," Bree says sweetly.

Oh, good god, here we go. Laughing, I hug each of them. They put their orders in and come sit down. I can tell them all at the same time. "Ladies, I love that you drop whatever you are doing to come be here for me, but I know you have your own lives to live and businesses to run."

Hillary looks at me and says, "Nonsense. You are the most important thing today and possibly tomorrow, so spill. How do you feel? What do you need? The real question is, do you want me to kick Jackson's ass. You know I was serious about that."

Laughing, I say, "First of all, I love you, Hill, and, no, don't kick his ass...at least not yet, even though I think you could probably take him due to his fear of you. But I just saw *you know who* and I feel okay. I'm obviously not fixed, things are not going to change in an instant, but we have a plan of attack. Want to hear it?" I pause to look at my circle of friends and smile. I love these women, and they love me.

"I have some homework to get me in a forward-moving motion. The goal is to find my self-worth again, and in doing so, that should bring me some balance and happiness in my life again. So, my first assignment is to either talk to Jackson or, if I can't get my words out, I can write him a letter about how I feel. I think I am going to talk to him. Our communication is not the problem, so I think in person is best."

They all shake their heads, agreeing with me. Sam says, "I agree, and I think everyone else does. Open communication in a marriage is a must and since that isn't an issue for you guys, just talk to him. Plus, I think it will be better to see his reaction. Writing things down sometimes can take a tone itself and be interpreted wrong. In-person is definitely the route to take. Continue, please."

"The second assignment is to journal my thoughts and reactions to things. What makes me happy, sad, angry, and then when I go back, we will discuss ways to move forward with those things that happen in my life."

Bree smiles, "Jules, I journal every day. Sometimes I just jot down a moment that makes me smile or write about something I saw that grabbed my interest. It's nice to have it written down to where you can go back and reflect on it if needed."

"I haven't written in a journal since I was a little girl and wrote in my diary. Of course, having two brothers who found my diary and broke it open with Dad's tools had my diary writing come to an end, but I agree that it won't be something difficult to do. At least, I hope not. Along with journaling. I must take an hour of Me Time. This hour must be where I am doing what I want, not something for someone else. This can be part of what I write about in my journal because I need to keep track of what and when I take Me Time."

Taking a deep breath, I look at my besties, "The last assignment is the biggest - five dates. Jackson and I must go on five dates. At least one every week starting this weekend, and it has to be a priority for us both."

Hillary jumps up and throws her hands in the air, "YES! I love this, and I am going to increase your odds."

I look at Ellen. "Um, Hill, do I dare ask what the hell you are talking about."

Feeling all kinds of proud of herself, Hill looks at all of us and says, "Oh, Jules, you two can't be the ones making the dates. I mean, if Jackson plans something, and then it's a flop, that represents Jackson failing again and vice versa. So, being the genius I am, I will assign your first date. Once you have date number one tackled, I will pick the next person to assign date number two and so on."

Glancing around the table, I see nothing but smiles and excitement. I think Hill has a solid point. Jackson and I are a couple, but we belong to a large group of the same friends. This situation seems to cross over into their lives, so why not. How bad can it get to let them pick and plan our dates? I tell myself that it can't be that bad, with just a hint of doubt but more excitement.

∞∞∞

After my stop with the girls and discussing my assignments for

Dr. Rose, I head over to Jackson's office. It is almost four o'clock, and I know he is still in his office seeing patients.

"Hi, Paige, is Jackson with a patient?"

Paige smiles at me, "Hi, Julia, it is so nice to see you. Yes, he is in a room right now. He has a couple more patients today and then should wrap up. I can snag him between rooms if you want?"

"That sounds great. I won't take up much of his time because I need to get home for Josie. Please let him know I'll be in his office." I walk to the office and open his door. He has files on one side of his desk, most likely from all the patients he needs to document from today and file. His office is filled with pictures of our family and us. I sit in one of the chairs in front of his desk and wait.

Chapter Ten

Jackson

Putting the patient's chart back in the door for Paige, I turn as I hear her coming toward me. "Paige, this patient is going to check out and needs to schedule a follow-up in two weeks. I made the notes on his file."

"Jackson, Julia stopped by and is in your office if you have a chance to see her before you go into your next patient."

Surprised to hear my wife is here, I immediately went to my office. I hope she's okay and that nothing has happened to someone in the family. Opening the door, I see her sitting in the chair, scrolling her phone. When she hears me, she looks up and smiles. "Hi, honey, is everything alright? I'm surprised to see you today, and now you have me worried."

I watch her as she looks at me, and her smile falters. "No emergency, but I did come here to talk to you. I won't take too long because I know you still have patients to see. I want you to make sure you are home tonight. We need to sit down alone and talk. I went to see a therapist today and need to talk to you about it. We need to talk about why I felt I needed to talk to her about a separation and what I need to do next."

Standing there just staring at my wife, I don't even know what to say to her. What the hell does she mean that she went to a therapist today without my knowledge and that there is more to discuss and things she needs to do? "Julia, first, I want to tell you that I love you very much and work hard to ensure you and the kids have everything you need. I'm glad you went to talk to someone if that will help you figure things out." I slowly sit in the chair next to her and take her hand. I take a deep breath and exhale. "I will make sure I'm home on time. Okay?"

She nods, smiles, and says, "Thank you. See you later."

I just sit there and watch her walk out of my office. Is my wife about to leave me? I put my head in my hands and rest my elbows on my legs. "What the fuck!" I say under my breath.

∞ ∞ ∞

Thank god there were no emergencies, and I got out of the office on time. I'm pulling into the driveway at five-thirty, and as I pull into the garage, I feel a sense of dread. Jules coming to my office to make sure I'm home so we can talk. That never sounds good. Okay, let's hear what is going on so I can try to make it better. "Jules, I'm home," I say as I walk into the house. Rounding the corner, I see her in the kitchen. She looks up as I approach. Her eyes are not right. Her smile doesn't reach her eyes, and the sparkle is missing. "Hi, it was a long week, but I'm glad it's over. Where are the kids?"

"They went out with Ellen and Scott for pizza. Ellen wanted kiddo time, and since I wanted to talk alone, it all worked out. Why don't you go grab a shower and get out of your work clothes, and we can have dinner together and talk."

I walk over and give her a kiss and a hug. "Sounds good, give me fifteen minutes, and I will be down," and head upstairs with a sense of doom hanging over my head.

After my shower, I head downstairs. Jules is still in the kitchen, pulling a dish from the oven. "Is there anything I can help with?"

"Jackson, can you get me something cold to drink with dinner while I make our plates? Then we can go sit down and eat dinner first."

I grab her ice water since I know she doesn't like to drink with dinner at home and help her carry the plates to the table.

We make small talk while we eat. She fills me in on how the week went with the kids and anything new with the family. What is completely missing so far is anything about herself. The big elephant in the room that is about to sit on me.

Cleaning up from dinner, she asks me if I need anything else, and I say no. I'm ready for whatever I have coming my way, at least I hope so. Slowly, she grabs a paper and slides it towards me. The paper is face down, so I can't see what she has written on it. She tells me not to flip it over just yet. Oh, fuck, what is happening! Is she sick, leaving me? What the hell is about to knock me out of this chair? It can't be good if she got rid of the kids being home for this talk. I take a deep breath, "Jules, you're really freaking me out. I don't know what to think, so obviously, my head goes to the worst-case scenario. Please, honey, please just talk to me. We can handle anything if we just handle it together."

"Jackson, I went to see Dr. Rose today because I am not happy. I am so lonely, and our marriage is in big trouble. I thought I needed us to separate." She puts her hand up. "Please, please, let me finish, and then I promise we can talk. Let me just get it out first, okay?"

What the ever-living hell is going on? What does she mean that she is lonely, and our marriage is in trouble? How? I do everything for her and my kids. What am I missing here? I need to calm down, or I won't even get through this lovely fucking talk of hers. I nod for her to continue because I better not say a damn word right this minute.

"I went to see Dr. Rose because I feel like I have no self-worth anymore. Everything I do is usually for someone else. I make no time for myself; we make no time for ourselves. When is the last time we went out, or for that matter, had sex?"

Shit, now she wants me to talk. "Well, we went to your parents' Sunday for family dinner. I believe we had sex not last Saturday but the one before." God, that sounds awful. Am I too tired to even make love to my wife?

Sighing, Jules tips her head to the side, studies me, takes

a deep breath, and reaches for my hand. "Exactly, Jackson. We schedule our love life; we never make time for just the two of us anymore, and you're never around for us to have uninterrupted family time. Your work-life balance is totally skewed, and we're all starting to suffer from it. When you aren't working, you're so exhausted—you aren't with us one hundred percent. We need to make some changes before the damage is too much to overcome."

I look at my beautiful wife and now see the sadness in her eyes. I can tell she is holding back tears; even Duke has crawled up and laid by her feet. "Jules, I'll do whatever it takes to make you happy. I am so sorry that you feel forgotten and that you are lonely, honey. I guess the number of emergencies and patients have increased a lot lately. What do you want to do? What can I do?" How did I let things get so bad without even realizing what I was doing to my family? I will do anything to keep our family a unit and strong.

She looks at me, determined. "Okay, turn that paper over, and we'll discuss it. I love you, Jackson, but we need to start making some changes because I don't think our family can keep going in this direction. So, this paper is my homework."

I turn the paper over and see a list of things with comments and all kinds of doodles. Let's see what we have. The list reads: talk to Jackson, Julia's Me Time, and Journaling, five dates, and communicate—in all caps. I look up, and I'm starting to see the sparkle in her eyes try to reappear. Whatever it takes, I'm in.

"The first thing is to talk to you, which I have. Our communication has normally been good, but I started feeling so angry with you. Every time you miss a gathering with friends or family, not making time for the kids, it leaves me feeling like you just didn't see me anymore. I would get sad, lonely, and then always so damn angry. I felt like I wasn't a priority for you. The kids weren't a priority for you. Do you realize how often a patient or emergency took you away from us after office hours or on the weekends? It just got to a point where I was hoping you would notice. You look so exhausted when you come home some nights. I just hoped that you would recognize how things were without me having to hit you over the head with it. Now I'm sorry that I let it get to this point. That I didn't say something to you from the beginning. I will own that, but now that I am talking to you, I also need to ask you to own your choices and make changes to how you live. I can't do that for you, Jackson. You need to figure out a better life and work balance. That is your homework, okay?"

Running my hands through my hair, I think about how I'm a giant asshole. I thought by working myself to the bone. I was providing for my family and doing enough. I now realize that I was providing for them, but I wasn't nurturing them or even being part of my family. I am not a guy that cries but man. I look up, and Jules is staring at me and rubbing her thumb on my knuckles, looking concerned, biting the corner of her lip.

"Jules, anything. I am such an ass. I didn't realize I was letting you and the kids down. I knew at times I missed things, and Daniel would give me the silent treatment. Josie has been trying extra hard to be near me when I have been home. I am so sorry. I have been taking care of everyone else but my own family." A few tears that I can't stop roll down my cheeks, and she uses her thumb to wipe them away and then leans forward and kisses me softly. I love this woman with my whole soul.

"We can fix this, Jackson, but we must work together and be a team again. So, the next thing on the list is Me Time and journaling. Dr. Rose wants me to take an hour a day to do something I want. Other people can be involved in my Me Time, but it must be my choice and something for me. Then she wants me to keep a journal and talk about each day. I can decide if I want to share the journal entries with her at my next appointment, or it can just be for my benefit. She said it will help to get my thoughts down in the journal and then be able to review them later."

"That sounds like a good idea. What does Me Time involve exactly? Pampering and alone time?"

"Exactly, or if I want to go see a movie that I want, it would be fine if you and the kids went with me, but it would be an activity that I wish to do. And if I want, I can also do it myself," she says and smiles.

I look down at the paper, and next is five dates. That seems simple enough. I can handle that, although her smile seems to have grown slightly more. As a matter of fact, she looks like she has a surprise in store for me.

"The next thing on the list is five dates."

Smiling, I grab her hand, "That is easy. We always have a good time when we go out together. I look forward to it."

Oh god, he is going to kill me and be upset that I talked to the girls before him, but he knows they are my girls and my best friends. Of course, I went over how I was feeling with them and what I was going through. "So, Jackson, yes, five dates, although they are not just any dates."

Looking at my wife, she is back to looking nervous. She has a tell when she bites the corner of her lower lip. "Jules, why do I feel like I may not like this part?"

"So, I may have talked to the girls a little bit about how I was feeling before and the whole thing after my appointment with Dr. Rose. After getting to the five dates part of my homework, Hill kind of hijacked the first date. She is going to tell us what our date is going to be and where."

I sit there looking at my wife. I'm glad she has girlfriends she can go to when she needs to vent and talk, but I don't really like that everyone knows our business. Whatever happened to 'what happens between a couple stays with that couple,' not stays with all best friends.

"Jules am I a little upset about you talking to the girls, yes, but not because you didn't come talk to me. Now everyone is going to be into our business. I already feel like an ass knowing I let you down, and now they're all going to think I'm an ass."

"Honey, everyone else was already clued in on our business because they could see through my mask better than I thought. Honestly, when I first said something to the girls, they talked me out of asking you for a separation. Ellen was the one that referred me to Dr. Rose, and they all told me not to make a rash decision."

Fuck, she was going to leave me. I'm such a jackass. "So, I should actually be thanking them for saving our marriage and pointing you to Dr. Rose? I guess that is a much better way of looking at the situation. But Hill, Jules! Come on. God knows what she will do with this date she hijacked."

Chapter Eleven

Julia

It's Thursday morning, and I'm enjoying my coffee on the porch with Duke at my feet, snoring. I'm thinking about how well my talk with Jackson went last night. I was so nervous to tell him how I've been feeling. That I was unhappy and had lost my self-worth, but he was there for me one hundred percent. I know he was upset, but he listened and agreed we need to make some positive changes. Did he really have no clue how lonely and lost I have been feeling? Men! *Thumps chest* I am the provider; I kill animal for food! *thumps chest again* Ugh, sometimes they are so stupid. Huh, what is going on? I can hear my phone buzzing nonstop. Oh no, Hill is doing her damn group text again.

Hillary: Our beautiful Jules and idiot Jackson need our help!!!
Hillary: Homework: Five Dates. I get to plan Date #1
Hillary: WHEN? This Saturday Night
Hillary: WHY? Lost Mojo-need it back *Sad emoji*
Hillary: WHAT? Goodwill Date
Jules: Hill, who all is on this group text???
Rob: Me
Garrett: *Thumbs up emoji*
Ellen: Hi
Bree: Me too *Hand emoji*
Sam: Paul and I *wave emoji*
Scott: Me too
Coop: Thanks Hill *Annoyed emoji*
Scott: Hey
Jackson: Oh shit-seriously Hill??
Hillary: Yep, suck it up, buttercup
Stella: *daisy emoji* hi
Julia: Why did I agree to this UGH
Rob: Tell me more...what is this about???

Bree: Be nice Rob---please

Hillary: You are ALL on here because we are their only hope, their closest friends or family and we need to hold J&J accountable

Hillary: Boys, you get Date #2 so shut it a sec

Hillary: Date #1 Challenge

Jackson: Oh fuck, Jules???? Control your friend pls

Hillary: shh!

Hillary: Goodwill Challenge Part 1

Go to Goodwill

Spend less than $10 each on clothes for each other to wear

Create names and backstory for your new appearance

Hillary: Goodwill Challenge Part 2

Provide your 'Support Team' (all of us) photographic evidence of outfits and date throughout the evening

Rob: OMG, I fucking love this!!!

Garrett: Please don't get arrested, as sheriff this would humiliate me

Jackson: And this won't humiliate me?

Coop: Please do not come to Cooper's Corner

Garrett: Second that ^^^

Sam: This is hilarious. Can I know where you go so, we can watch?

Julia: No. My rule is none of you participate or the deal is off

Jackson: what my beautiful wife said ^^^

Rob: Suck up!

Cooper: *laughing emoji*

Ellen: This is awesome. Hill for the WIN!!!

Hillary: Better go get your outfits before your date Saturday

Stella: This is SO romantic and I will hang with Josie *Smiley emoji*

Jackson: CHALLENGE ACCEPTED

Julia: What he said ^^^^^^ *heart emoji*

Chapter Twelve

Julia

It's Friday night, and the kids gave us an hour to run to Goodwill and find our outfits. Daniel and Josie are making us spaghetti dinner while we go find our outfits and create our characters. God let's hope no one sees us there doing this.

Jackson parks the car in front of Goodwill and looks over at me. "So, ten bucks max, we go in, find each other's outfit, pay, and meet back at the car. Right?"

Laughing, I shake my head yes. "Oh my god, Jackson, why did we agree to this? Should we act like we don't know each other inside, or should we do this together?"

"How about you go look for me, and I go look for you? If we need to try something on, we can. That way, we are only here doing this one time."

We get out of the car and just stare at the front of the Goodwill, look at each other and start cracking up. By the time we catch our breath, Jackson grabs my hand and says, "Let's do this!" with the most determined look on his face. Damn, my husband is hot! Off we go, and god help us.

I head to the men's section while he heads directly to the dresses. I'm looking through the racks of clothing and spot the most hilarious bowling shirt. Something that he would normally not wear. Shrugging my shoulders, I think why not and grab the blue with black stripe shirt for four dollars and ninety-nine cents. I have five bucks left to spend, and oh yes, I see the perfect accessory a few rows over, a fedora for two dollars and ninety-nine cents. Sold! I look up and don't see Jackson, so

I rush to pay for my purchases. A total of about eight bucks for his sexy outfit. I think the poor kid at the register thought I was nuts. I couldn't stop laughing through the entire purchase. Since I finished my purchase, I wait in the car.

Jackson

I'm digging through the racks of dresses, but I haven't quite found what I am looking for yet. Granted, we are shopping at Goodwill, not Macy's. Then I see it, a dress that Jules would probably never buy herself but would look sexy as shit wearing. She dresses more conservatively, we both do, and people joke that we walked straight off a Gap ad. We like what we like, so what's the big deal? I find a dress that is a sparkly black silver stretch mind—one of those dresses that fit like a tube and only has one shoulder with a cut-out pattern. I want to fist-bump the lady looking at dresses next to me because, ladies and gentlemen, we have a winner—and at the price of only five dollars and 99 cents!

I look around, but I don't see Jules. She must be done shopping for me already. Before I can walk to the register, the woman next to me stops and looks at me strangely. Does she think I am buying this dress for myself? I bet she does!

"I think this dress will look pretty on my wife, don't you?" She lifts her eyebrow at me. I smile and walk away. Awesome! Jules will love that story. I pay for the dress and walk out to the car. When my wife sees me heading her way, I almost fall over at the beautiful smile she gives me that finally reaches her eyes.

∞∞∞

We arrive home and the kids are in the family room watching a movie. "Hey, we're home. Ready to eat?" Jules ran our purchases upstairs after promising not to look in my bag.

Daniel is the first one in the kitchen and stops in front of me, "Did you guys find outfits for tomorrow? Uncle Rob sent me a text wanting me to find out where you are going for your date."

Sneaky bastard! "Uncle Rob should mind his own business. The deal was that we don't have to tell them where. We only have to share who and what."

Daniel looks at me and very seriously says, "Dad, don't mess this up. You best not have an emergency. I know what's going on. I talked to Aunt Ellen because she said I might need to be around the next couple of weekends to help with Josie. Don't let us down, okay?"

Heartbreaking. My own son knows what a fuck-up I've been, and I've obviously let him down too. He is growing into a strong man himself. "Buddy, the last thing in the world I would ever want to do is hurt you, Mom, or Josie, and I know I have lately. I am sorry, and I am going to try to do better."

Of course, Josie overheard everything, but my little peacekeeper does just that. She comes over to me and gives me a big bear hug. "Love you, Daddy. Are you excited about your date tomorrow with Mom?"

"I'm more excited than you can imagine. I hear you're hanging with Aunt Stella. What are you two planning on doing?"

"She said she doesn't want to interrupt your date, so I'm supposed to text her the minute you leave, and she'll come get me. We're going to go to the movies. There's a new Rom-Com out that we're both dying to see."

Chapter Thirteen

Julia

After dinner, we head upstairs to see what we bought for each other and start creating our characters. Jackson tells me to go first and show him what he will be wearing. "I picked out a shirt and accessories. You can decide what bottoms to put with it. I hand him his Goodwill bag, and he slowly pulls out the bowling shirt and fedora and starts cracking up.

"Jules, this is great, and, honestly, I was expecting the worst, and this isn't it. Hmm, so a bowling shirt and fedora—let me see."

I watch him as he starts pulling things from the dresser and walking into the closet. He comes back toward me and puts everything on the bed for me to see. "So, you are going to wear your blue bowling shirt with black stripes, your fedora, khaki shorts, tube socks, and sandals?" Oh, dear god, this man is really trying to make me happy. "Do you have a character in mind, or do I need to wait for him to appear tomorrow?"

Jackson looks at me, smiles, and with a German accent, says, "Ja Fraulein, I am Dieter, visiting from Germany. I like good beer and came to see the Magnificent Mile of Chicagoland."

I can't decide what is worse, the outfit or my husband's terrible German accent. I am laughing so hard that tears are leaking down my face. He walks over and grabs me around the middle, pulling me in tight to his chest.

"Jules, if acting like a guy with a bad outfit and horrible accent makes you laugh like this, I'll do it every day. I love you, and watching you laugh and be happy makes me want to do whatever I can to help this continue." Then he kisses me with hunger. Our kiss goes from sweet to a sensual all-consuming kiss. I pull away breathless and just stare at him.

"Jackson, wow, I love you, and I've missed you so much, missed us. Alright, I guess it's my turn."

Jackson hands me his bag, and I pull out what looks like a foot of fabric. "Jackson, where is the rest of it?" I look in the bag, and nope, that is it. Oh boy, time to step out of my comfort zone. What the heck is my husband up to?

"Before you get upset, I want you to listen to me. This is our chance to dress each other up. I know that this style is not something you would pick for yourself. It isn't even something I would expect you to wear, but now listen, please, I know if you put this dress on, it could give you a new attitude that inspires you. Plus, you'll look smoking hot!"

I stand there, stare at the dress, and even stretch it a bit. Laughing to myself, I look at my husband, lift my eyebrow, and head to the closet. I return with my stiletto heels, walk to the dresser, grab my jewelry box, and find the four-inch hoop earrings I wore for Halloween. I head towards the bathroom and bring out my red lipstick, then turn and look at my husband, whose eyes have gotten very excited and round.

With my best southern accent, I look over to my husband, "Sweetie, my name is Chardonnay, and I came up from Arkansas to visit a cousin in Chicago and just fell in love with the big city. I moved here to make it big on the stage!"

Walking back downstairs to join the kids for a bit before bed, we sat on the couch together. I pull Jules close to me and snuggle her into my side. I see both kids look over and watch us; then it feels like they both exhale and relax into the movie.

Josie smiles, "Are you guys ready for your date tomorrow? I can't wait to see what you bought for each other. This was a silly idea Miss Hillary had, but I hope you have fun together."

I smile at Josie. "I think we're both set, and you and Daniel are going to get a kick out of it too!"

∞ ∞ ∞

I'm eating my lunch on the porch with Jackson, who has been home since his return from the gym. I don't know what scheduling gods he spoke to, but I won't say anything to jinx it. Both our phones start buzzing, and Jackson's first reaction is alarm. He must think it's the hospital, but if my phone is buzzing at the same time, it can't be the hospital. I grab my phone and see text messages.

Hillary: Reminder that we will need photos of each of you, character bios and pics throughout the evening
Rob: I feel like a kid on Christmas morning I am so psyched for this
Bree: I hope you have an amazing night *Kisses emoji*
Garrett: Don't get arrested. I can't help you
Coop: Please don't come to Cooper's Corner
Sam: Paul and I can't wait to hear the character bio and deets
Ellen: Scott and I say ditto ^^^^^^^^^^^^^^^
Stella: So romantic and fun. Remind Josie to text me when you exit
Hillary: **Marvin Gaye voice * Let's get it on!
Julia: Characters & Outfits ready
Jackson: More to come later, much later

Chapter Fourteen

Julia

I'm upstairs getting ready for Date One, "The Goodwill Challenge," and I'm looking forward to the shenanigans tonight. We've already laughed more in the last two days than we have in months. I see Jackson is also enjoying it even though it seems silly. I get my hair poufy and full of hairspray as the best eighty's icon, and my makeup is dark and bold, especially the red lips. Now comes the time I stretch this child-size dress over my hips, chest, and ass. Please don't make me look completely ridiculous. I turn slowly and look at myself in the mirror, "Well, hello, Chardonnay, you sassy little sex kitten."

Putting on my heels and grabbing my little clutch purse, I head down the stairs. I will need a glass of wine before we leave the house looking like this. As I walk into the kitchen, Jackson looks up, and his jaw drops. I stop quickly. "Oh no, that bad?"

"Oh no...that good!" I stare at him as the biggest grin takes over his face from ear to ear. He makes a beeline toward me, and I put my hand up to stop him and shake my head no. I know that look, but the kids are home, and we are leaving. I point to the stairs, telling him it's his turn to turn into Dieter.

As he walks away, both kids are staring at me with funny looks on their faces. Josie thinks I look pretty, but I am not sure what Daniel thinks. I watch him as he tries to put the right words together.

"Mom, um, don't be offended, okay? You look different, but are you going for the chick at the end of *Grease* or a prostitute?"

I can't do anything but laugh at my son's comment at this point. "Dad picked this out for me. He thinks I need to step outside my comfort zone, and this is way out of it. Funny, but wait until you guys see and hear him come down."

Jackson

It only takes me about ten minutes to get my outfit on and head down the stairs to the kitchen. Jules is waiting for me with the kids, and when she sees me, she just starts laughing.

"Oh my god, Dad, that is the funniest frickin' thing I have ever seen you in. I've got to get pictures of this for the evidence. Wait, first tell me who you are supposed to be," Daniel says.

"Ja, hallo I am Dieter from Germany. I like cold beer and ze Chicagoland. I met Chardonnay at Joe's Diner, and we are to be married."

Josie and Daniel are laughing at me. For once, they need to see this silly side of their dad because lately, all they see is the exhausted one or none at all.

They keep looking back and forth at us and can't stop laughing. Man, my family needed this, and, as much of a pain in the ass Hillary can be, she may have done me a big favor.

"Oh, ja, children, we are off to enjoy ze date. I must take Miss Chardonnay to ze favorite place for dinner and dancing. Please take our photos so that you can share them with ze others. Smile, darling!" I hand my phone over to Daniel, and I grab Jules and hug her tight while he takes our photo.

We are in the car and I haven't stepped out of character yet. I did some research on Germany, so I have a lot I can talk about with Chardonnay tonight.

"Jacks, I mean Dieter, honey, where are we goin' for supper?" she says in a southern drawl.

"Ja, Chardonnay, we are going to ze China buffet. Did you know that you pay fifteen dollars and then eat all ze food?"

Let's hope we don't run into anyone. We may never live this shit down, thanks to Hill. We took our evidence pictures of the evening that we will share with the group text. We created our character bios on our way to dinner since we decided not to share the information until after our date. We talk about staying in the moment throughout the night and put both our phones on silent. I can't go completely dark since I'm a doctor, but I hope we get time to be uninterrupted with each other.

We go to the China buffet, eat our dinner, and laugh through the evening. Thankfully, we don't run into anyone who knows us, and we remain in character throughout the night.

After dinner, we head to the Freeze Hut for an ice cream cone. Now we are just pushing our luck that we will run into someone we know. Not to mention, it's close to Cooper's Corner. If I didn't know any better, I would think my wife was having a fun night.

We both get out of the car, and thankfully, there are only two people in line, and they look like teenagers. We walk up to order, and I start telling the boys about Germany and that they should visit one day. We order our ice cream cones and sit at the bench that looks out onto Lake Harmony. I pull Jules in close with one arm wrapped around her and she lays her head down against my shoulder. Staring out on the lake at sunset is one of our favorite things to do.

"Are you cold, sweetheart? Do you want to eat in the car?"

"No, Dieter, let's sit here and watch the sunset and maybe after it's dark a shooting star. If we see one, we can make a wish."

Chapter Fifteen

Julia

When we arrive home, Stella and Josie must still be out, and Daniel is nowhere to be found. We walk into the kitchen, and I see a note on the counter from Stella-*House is all yours tonight. Daniel went to a friend's house, and Josie is bunking with me. Girls' night and snuggles for me! Love you two - enjoy alone time.*

I feel Jackson reading the note over my shoulder, his breath near my ear, "My lovely Chardonnay, it seems Dieter gets to have you all night. Let's go upstairs, and I let you yodel for me, Ja?"

Turning in his arms, I smile at my husband, "Dieter, you are just the sweetest man and sunshine of my sky. Please show me to your room and take my breath away."

We walk hand in hand up the stairs to our bedroom, where my husband pulls me in close. His hand brushes my cheek, and his eyes focus on me. "I love you so much, Jules, and I don't ever want to lose you. I had so much fun with you tonight." He leans forward and kisses me, and then pulls me in tight. His grip on me is like a vice, and he is consuming me with his mouth and hands on my back. His hands move to my hair, and then he backs up a bit, laughing. "Honey, I love you, and our night is not even close to ending, but I think your hair has turned into a rat's nest. How about we start this in the shower and clean ourselves off before bed? Plus, I really want to unwrap you from this sexy dress. I've been hard since I saw you walk into the kitchen."

"I'm all yours, Jackson. Help unwrap me, please."

He kneels, slowly takes one stiletto off, and then rubs his

hands from my foot up my calf and kisses my thigh. He moves over to the other shoe, repeats taking off the shoe, allowing his hands to wander north, and kisses me on my thigh. He pauses to look up at me and sees that I'm watching him and smiles at me. That smile is the one I fell in love with when we were young. He moves to the bottom of the dress and slowly rolls it up my thighs. Once he reaches my panties, he stops, and I hear a little gasp. Yes, I may have gone to the store and made sure if the night went how I'd hoped, he would have a lot more unwrapping to do.

"Jules, did you get me a special treat tonight? You know that blue silk happens to be my favorite." He leans in, smells me, and then runs his finger up my slit. "Are you wet for me, Jules?"

"Yes, Jackson. Can't you tell?" He continues to tease me by kissing me on my thighs and running his finger against my slit every so often. Then he pulls the fabric to the side, runs his tongue up my slit, and sucks on my clit.

"Baby, you are so wet for me. I am going to make sure you know how much I love you. I'm going to fuck you until you pass out tonight."

Standing up, he resumes the unwrapping of my body. He rolls the dress up and over my head. I am standing there in only my panties and matching bra. We just stand there a moment. Our gazes lock on one another.

"You are the most beautiful woman I have ever seen, and I am the luckiest man in the world to call you mine." With that, he pulls me in tight, and our kisses turn frantic, almost damaging. The heat between us is electric and unstoppable.

I pull away to take a deep breath, and then he pulls me in for another earth-shattering kiss. "Honey, I want to unwrap you too. It's only fair that we both take our clothes off." I start to unbutton his shirt and then let it fall to the ground. My hands move to his pants, and I slide his zipper down. My hand brushes his hardness, and I hear a soft hiss from his lips. He is so hard I can feel him pulsing against my hand.

Next, I bend down and push his boxers to the floor. I slowly slide my tongue up his cock and suck his head into my mouth. I use my mouth with my hand to suck my husband and listen as I hear his breathing change. I take my hand, move it to his balls, and squeeze a little bit.

He pulls me up from under my arms, "As much as I want you right here right now, we need to get this makeup off your face, and your hair washed first. Come with me." He takes my hand and walks us into the bathroom. He lets go of my hand and reaches behind my back to undo my bra, cupping my breasts as he pushes the straps down my arms. Then he takes his thumbs, slides them into the sides of my panties, and slowly drags them down. With both of us naked, he turns on the shower and walks into it, pulling me behind him. He hands me my face wash so I can get this makeup off my face before I look like a raccoon. Once my face is clean, he tells me to turn around and puts my head under the shower spray, wetting this mess of hair. Once my hair is wet, he switches places with me and puts shampoo in his hands. He starts to wash my hair and massages my head in the process. "Honey let's rinse your hair out. Switch places with me and tilt your head back."

As he rinses my hair, he leans forward and starts to kiss my neck, giving little nips and bites along the way. He slowly moves down and starts kissing my breasts. Moving from one breast to the other and giving each one the same beautiful attention. I am so wet and on edge. I grab his head and hold him to my breast as he takes my nipple into his mouth and sucks hard. I gasp from the sensation shooting from his mouth all the way down to the heat between my legs. He stands back up, smiles, and reaches for the conditioner. He applies a small amount to my hair and massages it into my scalp. I have no idea when I got this treatment from my husband last, but he is making sure I feel treasured tonight.

"My turn Jackson, let me wash you." I just want to get my hands on my sexy husband. For a forty-five-year-old, he is in great shape. He still has cut abs and that beautiful vee shape and hairline that runs down to his cock. I lather up my hands and begin to wash his hair. He moans as I rub his head, and I watch as the stress seems to fall away. I lean forward and give him a soft kiss on his chest. After rinsing his hair, I grab his body wash and smell the bottle. This is Jackson, the scent strong and musky and makes my knees weak. I soap him up slowly, running my hands over his chest and back. I let my hands fall to his cock, which is standing hard against his stomach, and wrap my hands around him. I move my hand slowly up and down his cock as he groans.

He opens his eyes and stops my hand and rinses off. "Not yet honey. I want to taste you first." He pulls me out of the shower, wraps a towel around my body, and grabs one for himself. He then takes another to dry my hair. Once we are dried off, he walks me over to our bed. "Lay down on the bed."

I do as he asked and go lay down on our bed and watch as he stands at the edge of the bed just looking at me. He smiles and comes down onto the bed next to me. He gives me a gentle kiss while his hands roam down my body. His kisses start to move down my body, lighting my senses on fire. His tongue licks around my nipple on one breast, then he nips my nipple and sucks hard. He then moves to the other breast and repeats the same, lick, nip, and suck. My wetness is building between my legs, and he knows how much he is turning me on. He reads my body after all these years and gradually moves his hand down, inserting fingers into me.

Slowly he moves his fingers in and out of me but never touches my clit. I start rotating my hips, trying to move him where I need him. I hear him chuckle because he knows he is putting me on edge and not letting me fall. His mouth starts moving down, grazing my thighs with his stubble, and I finally feel his tongue licking up my slit and my folds. His fingers continue to build my arousal, going faster and harder. I am so close to falling, but he knows how to edge me out and is enjoying this. "Jackson. please." He finally sucks on my clit, and I go falling over and into bliss. He moves slowly back up my body and over me.

"I love you, baby, and I will always love you."

I feel him as he pushes into me in one slow thrust making

me feel full. "Oh god, Jackson, I love you, but please, start moving." He begins to thrust into me, kissing me with passion and eagerness. He rotates my hips, gets an even deeper angle, and hits that spot. That special spot that has me seeing stars. "Yes, right there. Don't stop. Please, Jackson, harder."

He knows my body and can feel that I am on the edge and almost ready to orgasm again, so he thrusts faster and harder, gripping my hips hard. I begin to tighten around him, and as I cry out, he falls over too allowing my orgasm pull everything out of him. We feel as one, and I know if I lose this connection with my husband, it will devastate me.

"Jackson, promise me that we will live every day, making sure to tell each other how important we are to each other, and love each other with all that we've got."

Chapter Sixteen

Julia

Jackson and I slept wrapped around each other all night. We made love two more times before crawling out of bed this morning. Every time he moves past me, his hand will graze me, or he gives me a kiss. We connected again last night, and things feel good this morning. We decided around midnight to send off our pictures and character evidence to everyone before falling into a deep sleep. I hear my phone buzzing over on the counter, so I grab it and see a bunch of text messages. "Honey, let's look at these texts together." We snuggle together on the couch, and I open the group text.

Hillary: Well done lovebirds
Rob: Those pics were awesome! Still laughing
Coop: Thanks for not coming to Cooper's Corner
Bree: Aw, so cute guys *heart emoji*
Sam: Paul and I are almost inspired
Paul: No Hill, not a chance
Ellen: *heart emoji* *laughing emoji*
Stella: Is it safe to bring Josie home-text me good eta *wink emoji*
Garrett: Looked like a good time
Garrett: Check FB *worried emoji*

I looked over at Jackson, worried. "You open it. We didn't see anyone, did we?" Jackson opens Harmony Hears on Facebook and starts laughing, turning his phone to show me the post.

<u>Local Sweethearts With Personality Disorder</u>
Local couple was seen out around town last evening wearing what we can only hope was meant for a costume party. Both

parties were seen wearing odd clothes paired with a horrific-mismanaged foreign accent. Were these love birds forced into this crazy appearance, or was this debacle by choice?

After reading and laughing together about Gertie's post online, we decide to make it a family day. I send Mom a quick text telling her we won't be at Sunday dinner later and will check in with her tomorrow. Once the kids come home from their overnight stay, we decide to make homemade pizza for dinner and watch a movie together. He is really making a solid effort with the kids and being present again. I am thankful that he seems to understand how much time we have spent missing him lately.

"Jules, did you get any 'Me Time' today?"

"No, but that's okay. I have enjoyed the afternoon with you and the kids."

"Josie wants me to help her make some cupcakes for dessert, so why don't you go relax and take a bath with your book for an hour. I'll be here to handle the rest while you take some time for yourself."

I stare at my husband and smile. As I get up and go to walk upstairs, he grabs my hand, pulls me into him, and gives me a kiss. As I pull away to head upstairs, he smiles and winks and tells me he loves me. *I love you too, honey, so much.*

While upstairs, I grab my journal because I want to make sure I get some things written down from our date last night and how things went this morning. Dr. Rose wants me to journal my feelings, so I need to make sure to get all the good and bad from my day. Thankfully, the last two days have been overflowing with good. I laugh to myself thinking of his ridiculous accent and how he talked to the boys at the Freeze Hut. If I am not mistaken, I think both of those families are his patients.

Finishing up with my journal, I fill the bath, slowly sink into the lavender water, and close my eyes with a sigh and smile.

Chapter Seventeen

Julia

After the kids head off to school and I sit on the porch with Duke sleeping at my feet, the doorbell chimes. I'm not expecting anyone, and since I am barely awake, I hope it isn't an emergency. I open the door to Mom standing there with a smile and invite her in. "Hey, I wasn't expecting you. Is everything alright?"

"Morning, honey, that's why I'm here and what I came to find out. Let's go sit down and talk. I think you've been holding some things close to your heart, and I want to make sure you're doing okay."

I grab Mom a cup of coffee, and we head back out to the porch to sit down. I explain how I am feeling about my husband, who works too much with the town growing and his emergencies taking over, the kids missing him and being disappointed often, and then tell her how I feel like I am everyone else's go-to for handling things for them, but that I don't have a purpose myself. I feel like I have lost my self-worth, and I am not sure what to do to find it and feel whole again. I tell her that I went to see Dr. Rose and that she is helping me figure out how to approach Jackson and my feelings about him never being present and taking time for myself to try to figure out what it is that I need to be happy.

Mom grabs my hand with glistening eyes. "Honey, I am so sorry that you didn't feel comfortable coming to me and letting me support you. All I ever wish for my kids is to be happy and know that no matter how old you are, I'm always here for you."

"Mom, it has been building slowly, but I didn't want to rain on your parade while we were planning your big anniversary party. I couldn't share my sadness when it was such a special time for you and Dad. I'm okay. Dr. Rose and I have a plan in place. I have homework on how Jackson and I can try to reconnect and how I can take time for myself and not feel guilty doing so. I need to learn that it is okay to need time for myself and not just be there for everyone else. Mom, somehow, over the last couple of years, I have just lost myself. Yes, I am a mom and wife, but what do I have that is just for me? Something that I have control of and is just for my benefit. I can't even tell you what that is, but I am trying really hard to find it because I want to be happy and feel whole again."

"Honey, please know that I'm always here for you, and that is for sad and happy times. You can always lean on your mom for anything, so don't forget. Now, please tell me what the heck I am hearing about this date and why you were dressed and acting the way you were?"

Laughing, I shake my head and explain to her the homework from Dr. Rose and the five dates. I tell her that Hill hijacked our first date last night and what the challenge was about. Then I share all the photos we took and talk about the post Gertie made. By the time she leaves, I'm feeling better. Moms just have the magic touch. She is right when she told me it doesn't matter how old I get; she can help make me feel better.

We talk a little longer about life and what is going on with the rest of the family. We are both concerned about Stella but know she will be okay and find something that makes her happy. My brothers are bachelors of Lake Harmony that don't seem to be interested in ever becoming one part of a couple. The trip that we gave her and dad for their anniversary. As time wraps up and mom and I have lunch together, she leaves and gives me a big hug.

"I know you have to get ready for your appointment this afternoon, but as your mom, I just wanted to see for myself that you're okay. I heard about your date through the grapevine, and when you called to say you were skipping Sunday dinner, well, I just needed to see you with my own eyes so I'd be able to judge for myself how you are doing. I'm going to go now though because you do look better. Love you, honey, so much."

"Love you too, Mom."

$$\infty \infty \infty$$

It has been a week since my first appointment with Dr. Rose, and I'm both nervous and excited to talk to her and tell her how things went for my first week of homework. I have journaled, gone for a run or a swim for exercise almost every day, visited with mom, had coffee with the girls, and enjoyed some much-needed time with my husband or as a family.

During my appointment, we discussed that communication with Jackson over how I feel went well, our first date was fun, and we enjoyed each other and reconnected this weekend. I also told her how I'm taking 'Me Time' and why it sometimes makes me feel guilty. I know it shouldn't, but sometimes I do feel like there are more important things I could be doing. I suppose that attitude is why I'm feeling so out of sorts. Dr. Rose loved that my friends added that others must plan the date. She thought that was creative and that people who care about us may also ask us to step out of our comfort zone and try something new. Focus on really making the 'Me Time' happen and that I shouldn't feel guilty and journal why I do.

The guys are in charge of this week's date, and I haven't heard anything yet. I wonder what they have planned. I am sure it will be good because they will need to top Hill's super fun date. Everyone knows how competitive she is, and Garrett can be too, so this should be interesting.

Chapter Eighteen

Jackson

Sitting in my office during lunch, I get a knock on the door. I tell whoever is on the other side to come on in. I slowly see the door open, and Garret walks in wearing his Sheriff uniform. "To what do I owe this visit?" I watch him walk over to the chair in front of my desk and lower himself, slowly exhaling with a slow sigh.

Garret stares at me for a minute and then says, "What the fuck is going on, Jackson? I know you've been swamped at work lately and missing things because of patient emergencies, but to hear at our poker night through the friend grapevine that my sister was going to leave her marriage is not something I want to hear. So, what are you doing to fix this shitshow you have created? I know you said you were working on it and didn't have time to make changes, but please tell me that in the last week, that isn't the case anymore."

I am not surprised that one, if not both, of my brother-in-laws are up my ass for being a horrible husband and father lately. Garrett and I are closest since we grew up together and were friends all our lives but for him to drop in during the workday was a bit of a surprise.

"I know I've dropped the ball and haven't been around lately. Jules and I knew being the town doctor when I started this practice would possibly interfere a bit when I started my practice, but the town is growing, and so is my patient load. I am trying to figure out how to balance things, but I guess my focus was on providing for my family. I know it's gotten out of hand, and I'm working on it.

"The last thing I fucking want is to lose my wife. She and the kids are the most important things in my life. I'm trying to fix it. I'm making them a bigger priority, and we are working through this, I promise. You saw we did the Goodwill date Saturday, and we both had a great time."

I watch as Garrett slowly relaxes in front of me.

"Man, I don't like seeing Jules and the kids unhappy, so I'm glad you are making this a priority. Date two is up to the guys, so we need you to meet us tomorrow for lunch at Coop's. We're going to brainstorm to make it a better date than the last one Hill cooked up. I already talked to your front desk and made sure they know to push you out the door and not book you up around that time. See you tomorrow, man— don't miss it! I gotta handle the town square mess and see if Gertie has gotten any gossip on who screwed around in the fountain in the park. Sometimes having her ear to the ground comes in useful. Did you see her post about it?"

"No, I haven't even had time to enjoy a cup of coffee today."

Garrett pulls his phone out and hands it to me to read Gertie's latest post in Harmony Hears.

<u>Hoodlums Vandalize Beautiful Fountain In Town Square</u>
Last night, our beautiful fountain that sits in town square was spray painted, red dye dumped in the water, and the roses in the flower beds trampled. Shame on whoever took our town's pride and joy and turned it into an eyesore. Sheriff Stone is asking for any information on who is responsible for this tragedy—we're looking for you! Please see the sign-up sheet at Lansing Gardens & Design for cleanup crew duty. There will be a fundraiser announced soon to cover the cost of repairs.

As I walk into Cooper's Corner, I see all my buddies in the far booth. Coop's place is the main bar and grill in Lake Harmony, so he knows how to accommodate big crowds and has extra-large booths to fit a family of six when needed. As I walk up to the booth, I look around the table and see Julia's two brothers, Garrett and Rob, Coop, Paul, and even Scott. "Wow, how did I get so lucky to get all of you here at the same time?"

Rob, Julia's younger brother, looks at me with his usual smirk and says, "We have to up the stakes and plan better than the Goodwill Challenge date and come on, we can't let you fuck it up. Since we're in charge of this date, we're going all out and creating a grand gesture full of memories."

I sigh and sit down, looking around the table at all my friends. I need to get over the fact that everyone knows our business and that I have let my family fall out of being a top priority. I almost lost my marriage, and now these dipshits, my friends, are responsible for my next date. I'm almost afraid to ask what they have planned, but I agreed to this, so here we go. "Go ahead. Fill me in."

Garrett looks at me and says, "We are going to recreate a happy moment between you and Julia. We think we know what that moment is, but we need your input to make sure we get the details straight. You can be part of some of the planning, but we are deciding what goes. Got me?"

"Yep, I'm all ears. I accept any help I can get, guys."

Smiling and rubbing his hands together excitedly, Garrett says, "We were thinking about the time you proposed to Jules."

I smile and lean back in the booth. "That sounds perfect. What do you need from me?" We talk through lunch and worked out all the details. I'm going to recreate the day I proposed to Jules and remind her why she said yes. As we finish lunch, Garrett takes out his phone and starts the group text. I hear everyone's phones around the table begin to buzz and watch as we all take out our phones to follow the text chain.

Garrett: Date 2- Remembering Why
Hill: Why what? Why we allowed the guys to plan this date?
Julia: Hill, be nice. Go ahead pls.
Rob: Thank you Jules. This is gonna be great!

Bree: *heart emoji*
Sam: listening
Garrett: The Guys (with me) have planned the next date
Garrett: When-Saturday afternoon
Garrett: More details coming directly to Jules from Jackson
Julia: Yay! *smiley heart wink emoji*
Stella: Cute
Hill: I think we deserve to know more details
Garrett: Nope, not yet-patience young grasshopper
Hill: Garrett! Don't start
Julia: Alright children no fighting
Jackson: what she said^^^
Rob: We are going to make this date even better than the last
Hill: Go ahead and try
Bree: Remember we need evidence
Stella: So Romantic *heart emoji*
Ellen: If Josie needs a date-LMK

Chapter Nineteen

Julia

Saturday, I wake up and get ready for the usual morning coffee with the girls at Harmonious Bites. When I walk into the kitchen on my way out, I see a huge bouquet of white lilies and a card sitting against the vase. I smile, lean over, and smell the flowers, which are my favorite because they smell the house like cinnamon. He is really trying hard to make me happy. I open the envelope and find a handwritten letter instead of a card.

Jules,

I hope that you slept well last night. When I woke up this morning, I just watched you sleeping so peacefully, and my heart was bursting with the love I have for you. I will make sure that you never forget how much I love you and need you in my life every day. I hope your day starts with a smile as you find these lilies, I bought for you. It was so hard keeping them hidden in my car last night, but I wanted you to wake up and know how much I love you and that I cannot wait for our date later.

I will be out of the house this morning setting up for our date. The kids know what I am doing and are with me. Yes! Can you believe they woke up early on the weekend to help me 'do it right!' They are sworn to secrecy, so don't bother asking them when they come home. Bribes won't work either!

Date: Dress for boating and casual dinner by the water. We can drive together to the lake. Bring a sweater in case it cools off after sunset. The kids are going to hang out with my parents for dinner.

Please take your time and enjoy coffee with the girls. Come home and relax, get your 'Me Time' in, and know that I love you with all my heart. I hope today helps you remember just how much.

Love you, J

Smiling to myself, I grab my purse and head out the door to Harmonious Bites to meet the girls for coffee. We try to have a standing Saturday morning date and whoever is free meets up. I can't wait to tell the girls about the love letter and flowers. He is bringing his game now. I feel like I'm seeing glimpses of the man I married twenty years ago. He always was a romantic and left me flowers or love notes I would find.

∞∞∞

Walking into the shop, I smile and wave at the girls in the back. I must be the last one to arrive. After ordering my coffee and grabbing a blueberry scone, I head back to the girls. "Good morning, ladies!"

"Wow, aren't you chipper this morning? Anything you want to share, Jules?" Hillary says with a smirk.

"Yes, I do have something wonderful to share. I woke up to a large bouquet of white lilies and a handwritten love letter."

Bree, our most romantic, sighs. "Oh, it must be so lovely to start your day that way. If only...."

"Aww, Bree, you aren't going to be single forever. You have so much love to share. You just haven't met the right one yet. It will happen."

Hillary laughs with the healthy skepticism we all know and love. "Just don't look for 'The One' online because that is just a shitshow."

Out of our group, Hillary and Bree are the only two left that are single. Bree is so afraid to date and make herself look bad since she is the town's Kindergarten teacher. Always worried about how her actions will affect her role in the community. On the other hand, Hillary doesn't care and will date anything she is attracted to. The only problem is they don't seem to be the right guy. We all know the right guy is usually right in front of her, but none of us know what happened between her and Garrett. Something did, but when and what we are not aware of, and neither of them is talking.

Ellen looks at me, "Are you excited about your date today? Date two-where is it happening?"

"I'm not sure. All I know is that we're going out on the lake today. He told me what to wear and to bring a sweater in case I get cold after the sun sets. I will keep you posted once I know more and, of course, share the evidence in photos."

∞∞∞

Jackson

Plans are in place for my date with Jules. The kids and I are heading to the dock to grab Paul's pontoon boat. Date two is recreating the day I proposed to Jules on Flynn Island. The island is a small, 2-acre spot towards the north end of the lake where people like to go camping or teenagers sneak away with their dates to be away from adult eyes. I'm going to set up a tent with a blanket, pillows, and candles for mood lighting and then grab the picnic dinner I had for us that night over 20 years ago. I smile as I remember that night when I proposed. We were so young, and both of us had such big dreams. Even back then, Jules supported me and my hopes and dreams and made it easy for me to achieve them.

As we boat out to the island, the kids are excited and talking about how happy they are that I've been around more lately. They offered to be part of setting up on the island and helping me get everything in place. Josie even sprinkled some flower petals around the tent's opening to make it romantic. I hope this doesn't get disturbed in the hours before I bring Jules back.

As I stand there looking at the setup for later, I see a guy walking over with a smile. He's wearing a Rolling Stones graphic t-shirt with jeans. "Whatcha doin' over here? I'm Carter, by the way," he says with a big smile.

"Hey, man, I'm setting up a romantic dinner for my wife. I'm heading home to grab the food, clean up and then head back with her. Are you going to be around for a bit?" He shakes his head yes, tells me he can keep an eye on things, and then heads back to where he must be fishing.

"Kids let's grab some lunch and order the food for Mom and I for our date later. That way, we can grab it on the way home. You're both heading over to Grandma and Grandpa's for dinner tonight, so you need to clean up too. Thank you for your help today. I sure hope Mom likes her surprise." I put my hand on Daniel's shoulder and said, "Thank you for your help today. I appreciate you spending the morning with me." He tries to hide the emotion in his eyes and nods, then turns away from me. *Baby steps.* I need to prove to my son that I am here and trying. I put my arm around Josie and squeeze my daughter into my side and kiss the top of her head. "Love you too, sunshine."

The kids and I head home to clean up, and I find Jules sitting on the porch with Duke reading a book. She looks so relaxed and peaceful. I'm glad that she seems like she has enjoyed her time today. "Hey, honey, how was your day so far?" She smiles at me and gets up to give me a kiss.

"I love my flowers. Thank you for thinking of me and remembering those are my favorite. I had a good day so far; coffee with the girls, time to swim, I wrote in my journal a bit, and now I'm relaxing with my book while Duke keeps me company."

"That sounds like a great day for sure. I'm going up to shower. I want to leave at about five o'clock and head to the dock. Make sure you dress comfy and bring a sweater. The temps may drop a little when the sun sets tonight." I lean over and kiss her before making my way upstairs. I sure hope Carter stays long enough for us to get back to the island. He seemed to be there for most of the day, so it should be okay. Who knows, maybe he's even camping overnight.

∞∞∞

Heading back to the dock with Jules in the car, I notice how cute she looks. She put her hair up in a ponytail for the boat ride and wore jeans that make her ass look great with a t-shirt. She also brought the summer sweater I recommended. We grew up in Lake Harmony and spent a lot of time out on the water. We both enjoy boating and swimming in this lake. I look over and grab her hand and she slowly faces me with a big smile that reaches her eyes. I hope I can recreate the night I proposed to her. I want this to be perfect tonight.

I have the same picnic dinner I brought for the proposal: fried chicken, potato salad, cornbread biscuits, and a six-pack of our favorite local craft beer. I laugh to myself thinking about how this was the meal I chose for our proposal picnic, but, at twenty-four, I suppose I thought more about my stomach than the ambiance of the moment. Josie made me throw in a couple of cookies for dessert.

We park at the docks, and I unload the food, grab my Bluetooth speaker for the music I downloaded on my phone, and try to keep Jules from peeking in the bags. "Come on now, don't be sneaky. You'll see what we're doing soon enough. Stop trying to look in the bags, honey." She smiles and gives me a shrug and giggles. We hold hands and walk to Paul's pontoon boat he let me borrow for the date.

She jumps right on and sits in the front seat next to the captain's chair. "Do you need me to help with anything, or am I just a passenger on this voyage?" She smiles at me and winks.

"Sit back and relax. We're heading out to the island, but do you want to drive around the lake first and enjoy ourselves? We're not in any hurry tonight."

"That sounds perfect! The sky is blue, and the sun is nice and warm. It should be a nice trip around the lake. Do you want me to grab you anything from the cooler?"

"Hey, I said not to be sneaky, and we won't be that long, so let's just go for a ride first."

We troll around the lake, pointing out The Yellow Lady Victorian home that sits up on the bluff. We always loved that house and wondered what it looked like inside. As we make our way over to Flynn Island, I watch Jules out of the corner of my eye and see the moment she spots the tent and our setup for the night. Her hand moves to cover her mouth, and I watch as she wipes away a tear that rolls down her cheek.

I park the boat on the shoreline, stand up, and pull her in my arms. "Honey, I didn't mean to make you cry. I was trying to bring back a happy moment for us."

Another tear slides down her cheek, but she is all smiles. "Honey, this is what you did for our proposal night. Is that the moment you want to recreate for me?"

Smiling, I lean down, wipe her tear away with my thumb and kiss her. "Yes, this is for us to remember why we promised our futures to each other. To talk about the dreams we had for ourselves, our future family, and to find a way to realign those dreams and make them into reality."

As we get off the boat and walk towards the tent and my set-up for the evening, I see Carter, and he waves to me and gives me a thumbs up. I wave back and then focus on the night ahead.

"Who was that?" Jules asks.

"Oh, Carter, I met him earlier when I was here with the kids. He came over and introduced himself and offered to keep an eye on things while I went home to grab you."

"That was nice of him."

We spent the evening enjoying dinner and talking about where we were in our lives after college and about to get engaged. We discussed how things were while finishing my Chicago residency and coming back to Lake Harmony to open a family practice. Jules' dream was to open her own business where she could work from home as needed once we started a family.

Somewhere along the way, we realized that my dreams had become a reality, and hers were pushed aside. She worked for Stone Builders and her dad after we were married and helped him with the growth of the construction business until Rob was old enough to partner up with her dad. Then she became a mom when Daniel was born, followed four years later by Josie. Her dream of owning her own business never happened.

"Honey, have you put any thought into what you would like to do now that the kids are older, and you don't really need to be home as much for them anymore? You always wanted to own your own business. Do you think that's something you want to do now that you have time?"

My beautiful and brilliant wife looks at me like I am crazy, her eyes big and her mouth open. I am doing everything I can not to chuckle. "Honey, what are you thinking right now because you're looking at me like I'm crazy."

She takes a deep breath, "Honey, that's kind of crazy. What in the world would I even do at this point? I haven't really worked in almost 20 years. I have a business degree, but I haven't thought of owning a business since college. What could I even do?"

God, I love this woman and even now, after being told to take time for herself, she still isn't sure how to even do that. "Well, what would you enjoy? You love to be active; you love working in the yard in your garden and flower beds, and you are amazing at organizing anything asked of you, does any of that sound like something you could turn into a business and enjoy? We don't have to worry about the financial piece of it right now, but what would make you happy? Maybe this is something to think about and discuss with Dr. Rose?"

After dinner, I pull out my phone and take a picture of us for our friends. They still want proof of date photos. Then I turn on some of our favorite songs, and we relax on the blankets and pillows the kids and I brought over and watch the sky darken and the stars appear. I got some firewood to make a small fire and light our candles to keep the bugs away. We sit there in our spot, snuggled together. Looking over at my wife with only the night sky and our campfire lighting our surroundings, I take the time to watch her. Her face is relaxed, and she is smiling and happily singing along with the music. She turns to me, and, without saying a word, I pull her into my arms and kiss her. A kiss that is not meant to be rushed but one that speaks a million words. My hands roam over her, and our kiss deepens and turns from soft and gentle to one of desperation. I trail my tongue down from her lips, across her jaw, and down her neck. She is hanging on to me tight, and her breathing quickens.

"I love you, Jules. I love you more today than the day I proposed. You have given me a life full of love, two beautiful children, and a large extended family."

"I love you too, Jackson. I never stopped. You've provided a life that I always dreamed of having. I just have missed you so much lately. I have felt so alone with you always missing moments with our kids or families. I know you love being a doctor and helping others, but I never imagined it would take you so far away from me. I should have spoken to you sooner about how I was feeling, but I felt guilty."

"Honey, everything I work so hard for is for you. If that is causing the problem, then I need to know so that I can make some sort of change. I've worked hard to provide a nice life for our family, but if working too hard causes me to lose the thing I am working for, then…. well…I'm not doing it right."

"I am so glad we've finally talked about this and made time to figure out how to move forward so that we're all happy and our family is healthy again."

I lean forward and kiss my wife, and once again, our gentle kisses turn into wandering hands and an urgent need for each other. I kiss down her neck as she wraps her leg around my hip and pulls me closer to her center. *Here we are, two grown people, fooling around on Flynn Island like teenagers.* I chuckle, and she leans back and looks up into my eyes, questioning me. I lean forward and kiss her slowly. We lay wrapped around each other, and before we forget where we are, we slow our kisses and smile at each other. "Honey, as much as I would love to take you right here like I did after our proposal, I would much rather enjoy you all night in the privacy of our own bed."

She bites my lip and laughs. "I agree. Let's pack up and get home."

As we lay in bed that night after making love, Jules curls into me and lays her head on my chest. "I've missed this, missed us so much, and I love how you are going along with the five dates and trying hard to make sure you're home more lately. I know how important your patients are to you, but it really has been nice to have you home with us."

"I know, honey, and even though you may not see it, I am working on things from my side too. I'm in this with you one hundred percent. Together we can fix it. Promise me you will think about the business idea, though. It may be what's missing in your life. The kids are older, more independent, and if you want to start your own business, I will help you in any way I can. I am completely here to support whatever you want, okay?"

"Maybe it isn't so crazy after all. Let me give it some thought. I'm not the person I was after college, and my dreams then don't fit into my life anymore, but I have some ideas. It's kind of exciting to think about."

I take her chin in my hand, "The real question, though, is, would you still say yes to my proposal if you could see where we are today?"

"Absolutely, I love you with all my heart. I wouldn't give up our life together or our beautiful children for anything. We just lost our way a little bit, but we're getting back on track. I love you very much, and my heart will always be yours."

Jules pulls me in for another kiss, and, like always, I just can't get enough of her. I kiss from her lips to her chin and up towards her ear, "I need more of you tonight." I move up, bite her earlobe, and hear her groan.

She whispers, "Take me then, but hurry because I need you now."

Chapter Twenty

Julia

Monday morning after the kids leave for school, I get a run in, shower, and head to the porch with my journal. I write down the details of our date on the island and smile. As I'm writing, I hear the doorbell, get up and walk to the door. I see my little sister staring at me with a big smile. "Hey Stella, what's up?"

Stella comes in and gives me a big hug. "Hey, I wanted to bring you a present. You always watch out for me and take my side when the family gives me a hard time, so I made you something to tell you how much I love you."

She hands me a pretty little gift bag as we walk in and head to the porch. "Do you want something to drink?"

"I'll grab it." She gets herself a glass of water, and we both sit on the porch swing. "Go ahead, open it."

She's smiling but looking a bit nervous and fiddling with her hands. I slowly glance into the bag and see a little jar, so I lift it out. It's one of those cute clip-lid glass jars with a pretty ribbon and a piece of lavender under the ribbon. It has a cute label on it that reads *Lavender Bliss Bath Salts*. "Oh! What's this, Stella? It's so pretty."

Twisting her hands and looking nervous, she says, "I've been playing around with some bath salts and homemade soaps. I worked with a lady in Sedona who taught me how to make salts and soaps using essential oils. I thought I could make these and see if anyone would buy them. You are kind of my guinea pig. I know you love to take your soaks in your tub, and lavender is your favorite, so I infused the salt with lavender oil and dried lavender. Do you...do you think you could try it and let me know what you think?"

"Absolutely! I can't wait!" This is a new direction for her again, but the bohemian, hippie sister may finally be on to something that fits her. I give her a big hug, "Stella, this is awesome. I love this, and you wrapped it up so pretty. Next time I take a soak, I will definitely use your bath salt."

Smiling and looking like a hundred pounds were pulled off her shoulders, she hugs me again. We talk for about an hour about other things she's making and trying with different smells and oils. She is excited about her new direction, and I can see the sparkle in her eye.

After Stella leaves, I am back on the porch thinking about what Jackson and I discussed. *Do I want to start my own business? What would I even do?* I saw how excited Stella was about her new business idea. *Is it really that easy?*

Chapter Twenty-One

Jackson

I'm sitting in my office adding notes to my patient charts I have already seen today. I grab my phone to send Jules a text message. I want to remind her that she is always on my mind and that I love her.

Jackson: Love you- hope you have a good day *heart emoji*

I see a notification from Facebook. Let's see if Gertie posted something about the fountain *hooligans*. Smiling and thinking about her constant gossip, I see that she has, indeed, posted something new.

The Yellow Lady Changing Hands
It seems that our lakeside Victorian, The Yellow Lady, will be on the market soon. Our favorite old-timers are ready to downsize and want to make sure she falls into the right hands. Who will be the lucky owner of a prized jewel on the bluff overlooking our beautiful Lake Harmony???

I walk into my next appointment after lunch and see that it is no other than Mr. Phillips, the owner of The Yellow Lady. *Has fate brought me this surprise?* "Good afternoon, Mr. Phillips. What brings you in today?"

"Dr. Harte, I was working on the house this weekend, and I seem to have hurt my shoulder. We're trying to clean out the house and go through all our things. We've decided to downsize and put the house for sale."

"I actually just saw that online. You know Gertie has her ear to the ground when it comes to things happening in town. Where do you think you will go? Are you staying around here or moving closer to one of the kids?"

"We're going to move a little further south, closer to our grandkids and away from the cold winters. The house is just too big for us now that the kids are all grown and moved out. We bought that place to raise our large family, and it was a great house, but it's time to make changes and enjoy the family we have before we get too old."

"Julia and I always loved that house. Growing up, we dreamed about owning it and raising our kids there. Having the shoreline so we could have a boat and private beach to enjoy right from home."

He looks at me and says, "Then, why don't you buy it from us?"

I stop examining his shoulder and look at him. I ask what the listing price is, and he says, "Dr. Harte, you grew up with some of my kids. I've known you and Julia all your lives. If you are interested, I know Marie and I would love to know it's going into good hands. We can talk numbers after you fix me up."

Julia is going to have a heart attack when I tell her I made Mr. Phillips an offer and that he accepted, and we are now the proud owners of The Yellow Lady. I have no idea what her plan is, but I couldn't let this opportunity pass. We must own that house. It was as if it was meant to be. *We can afford this. I have worked my ass off missing time with my family and friends. This was a good decision. Oh god, I hope she agrees with me.*

My phone buzzes, and I look down to see a text from Jules and smile as I read it.

Julia: Sorry for the late response. Stella stopped by. LOVE U TOO.

Chapter Twenty-Two

Julia

I have my appointment with Dr. Rose today, and I have a list of things I need to talk to her about: My own business, date nights, my marriage, and still trying to find my self-worth. *What is it that makes me happy? Where do I find that again?*

As I walk into the office for my appointment, the journal in my purse, my phone buzzes. I must have a text, so I pull out my phone.

Stella: This is your mom and dad - not Stella. We are using Stella's phone. We decided to jump in on this date planning and your dad and I get to plan the date for this weekend. You and Jackson have reservations at The Lighthouse restaurant at 7pm Saturday. Dress up! A romantic dinner for two and dancing. We are having the kids over for dinner and they can stay the night. Dad wants to go see some thriller movie with Daniel and I will make a date for Josie and me - no boys allowed! Remember, we love you both —have fun.
Rob: Nice text novel mom *wink emoji*
Stella: ROB! this is your Dad, don't be a wise ass to your mother
Garrett: Yeah Rob-shut it
Sam: Ah, I love the Lighthouse
Bree: Food is so good! *yummy emoji*
Hill: Not as good as my food!
Jackson: That sounds perfect mom and dad
Julia: Thank you both *heart emoji*
Ellen: Nice one mom and dad-bring the sexy on!

At my appointment, Dr. Rose and I talked about how things are getting better between Jackson and I, and how he is putting in the effort to be in the moment with us again. There have been some emergencies, but not too many, and when he is home, he makes sure to be present and involved. We also discussed the idea of me having my own business. Dr. Rose agreed that since I have this gap in my life where I have been trying to find my self-worth or purpose, putting some thought and effort into maybe having my own business would help fill that hole. She asked a lot of the same questions that Jackson did. *What makes you happy? What do you enjoy doing that you could make into a business?* I love doing parties and events for my friends and family. I also love working in the yard and my flower beds. I have some soul searching to do, but while I'm out. I need to stop by Sam's Garden Center. She got some new planters she thought I might want for the porch. Then I need to get ready for dinner at Jackson's parents' house. They're having us over tonight.

∞ ∞ ∞

The kids and I are at Jackson's parents' home for dinner. He is going to head straight here from work. We are all in the great room while we wait for my husband to arrive. The house phone rings, and his mom jumps up to answer. I watch her and know my husband is on the other end of the line as she says we will save him a plate. I look over at the kids, who are watching the exchange on the phone with their grandmother. They know it's their dad, and another emergency has come up, and he won't be coming to dinner.

Evelyn hangs up the phone. "Jackson got called to the hospital tonight. Let's go ahead and have dinner." She starts heading into the kitchen to get the food to the table, and I go and help her.

"Another emergency, huh?"

She smiles, "He is a busy doctor, isn't he? Let's eat before this roast turns into a brick."

∞ ∞ ∞

After dinner, we stay and talk a little bit longer about what the kids are up to, and the kids spill the news about how Jackson and I have been going on different dates. His parents had no clue I went to Dr. Rose and how bad things were at home between us. I'm done making excuses for him, so I don't. We get up to leave and head to the door. Everyone gives hugs to each other.

Evelyn hugs me and says, "Let's put something on the calendar again soon and hope Jackson can make it next time."

Both Evelyn and I hear Daniel say under his breath *Fat fucking chance.* I hold my breath as Evelyn looks at me with concern in her eyes. *What is there to say? He has let his kids down a lot. Me too!*

Evelyn pauses and looks up at me. "Oh no, Julia, I forgot to give you something. Can you come back to the kitchen for a moment, please?"

I tell the kids to go ahead and jump in the car and follow my mother-in-law into the kitchen.

Evelyn is standing with her back against the counter and her arms crossed in front of her. "Julia, dear, what the hell is going on with our son? Does he realize how he is putting his family in jeopardy? I heard what Daniel said out there. What can we do? How can we help you, honey?"

Taking a deep breath, "I know he has been working a lot lately and missing out on things. He didn't even make it to the party for my mom and dad, and he knew how important that was for my family. That night kind of set the wheels in motion. I lost it. I felt let down, and I was going to ask him for a separation.

"I look up and see her eyes get round, and her mouth open in shock. "Instead, I went to see a therapist to talk things out and try to find a solution to my family falling apart. That is when the dates started to try to reconnect Jackson and me a little more. I've also started trying to do things for myself without feeling guilty. We've been doing a lot better. This is the first emergency lately that kept him from coming home, and I think the kids just fell right back into that place of doubt. I will talk to them when I get home. We're okay. We're all working on it together."

"His father and I are going to have a talk with him. We both know what it is like, and I'm married to a doctor too, but he must find some work-life balance before he loses his family. It will be fine, honey. I am so glad to hear that you are both trying to fix things. Marriage is hard and a work in progress."

"Thanks, Mom. I know tonight threw a wrench in things with Jackson getting called in and missing dinner. The kids just want him to be around more. Thank you for dinner. It was delicious as always."

Two steps forward, one step back. That seems to be how things are going these days. Jackson makes an effort and spends time with us, and then an emergency happens with a patient, and it's like nothing ever changed. At least with the kids. I see he is trying, but our kids are not as forgiving.

Tomorrow is our fancy night out, and I'm looking forward to it. We haven't been out to a fancy night out for a bit, and we both love The Lighthouse. *I wonder what live music they will have tomorrow.*

∞ ∞ ∞

As I'm doing things around the house, my phone buzzes in the kitchen with a text. I head over and see I have a text from my husband.

Jackson: I left you something in the kitchen under your journal-go look

I walk over to my journal on the porch, and, sure enough, there is an envelope underneath. I open the envelope and find another handwritten note from my husband.

Jules,

I am so sorry that I missed dinner last night. I am excited about our dinner this weekend, and to make it even better, I set up some spa time for you and your sisters. I already spoke to Ellen and Stella and they are excited to go with you. You can go have massages or whatever you want. The girls will come pick you up late morning Saturday and spend the afternoon primping and relaxing.

I promised Josie a lunch date at Coop's, so that's what I'll be doing while you get some nice R&R with your sisters.

Love you, J

Chapter Twenty-Three

Jackson

It's still early morning, but I'm out of bed and about to head to the dock to meet up with Edison and my dad. They meet every Saturday when the weather cooperates and head out on the boat to fish with Peter. I grab my key, and on my way to the garage, I grab a notepad and scribble down a note to Jules and Josie.

Jules-Didn't want to wake you but gave you a gentle kiss anyway. Meeting Dad for breakfast this morning. Enjoy your day at the spa if I miss you. Can't wait to see you tonight!

Josie-lunch w me at Coop's. See you in a bit!

I stopped to grab a coffee and some extra sweet rolls on my way to the marina. I see Edison and my dad in the boat setting up their poles and cooler. No sign of Peter yet, so I may be able to get some time in with them first. "Hey, are you going out to catch dinner?"

They both jerk their heads toward me and laugh, "Well, look at you, joining the big boys at dawn to go fishing. Are you coming out with us or just stopping to say hello?" says my father-in-law.

"Well, that all depends on your wise knowledge and how quickly you tell me what else I can do."

My dad and father-in-law look at each other and after their silent communication, I get a response. "About time you come to us for help. What the hell is going on with you, and how do we knock some sense into you, son?" my dad says with a frustrated growl.

I explain to them how I'm always a no-show because of an emergency at the hospital. Julia and the kids are unhappy, and she went to therapy because she was so dissatisfied with our marriage and was thinking of leaving me. Obviously, this has been building for a long time because you don't ruin your marriage overnight unless someone else is involved, and we know that isn't the situation. Not unless you want to call work my mistress.

I talk about our five dates assigned by the therapist and the two we have shared so far. Edison starts chuckling and says he knows all about the dates and that he and Ruby planned date three for tonight.

"How do you know all the details about these dates?" my dad asks him.

Laughing, he says, "My kids have a group text chain. Stella shares it with Ruby and me, so we know what is going on. At least the texts about what's going on between Julia and Jackson and their dates. Then we jumped into hijacking the date idea and planned their third date. We're having them go to The Lighthouse for dinner and dancing tonight. We know it's their special go-to place for something important when they celebrate. We're hoping it puts the focus back on the two of them; not work, not the kids. If they can't find a way to be on solid ground again as a couple, nothing else will matter."

My dad agrees with Edison. I'm glad we have many people supporting us instead of making it worse. Dad says, "Thanks, Edison. I feel better hearing a bit more information on what's going on and how the kids are working through this. I think it's time I knock some sense into my son and have some father-son bonding. I'm going to skip fishing this morning and take my son to breakfast."

I look up as Peter makes his way down towards the boat. I hand over the bag of sweet rolls to him and Edison and tell them I will take a raincheck for fishing. Edison nods, knowing I am heading out with my dad for a serious talk.

∞∞∞

We both make our way over to the diner in our own cars to have a talk over breakfast. *This should be fun.* I see Dad sitting in a booth, already drinking coffee as he waits for me. I don't know how he beat me here. I take a deep breath and sit down. He raises his brow and stares at me like he did when he knew I was getting into trouble. He looks at me and watches as I slowly sink down into the booth and rub my hands over my face.

Taking a deep breath, I say, "Dad, I almost lost my family by having my head so out of focus I didn't even realize I was letting them down. Somehow by making sure I was providing for them and giving them the best that I could, I lost sight of the fact that I also need to give them myself and haven't been. Daniel is so angry that whenever I miss something because of work, he stops speaking to me. Josie tries to be the 'fixer' and hangs on me a little more like when she was a little girl. I have let both down and Jules. I've neglected her the most. Knowing she always had everything under control gave me a sense of permission to do what I needed to, so I worked, and worked too much. She wanted to leave me, Dad! I almost lost my family because my priorities got messed up."

My father listens with concern on his face. He takes his napkin and refolds it in front of him. He hasn't said anything, yet I know he is thinking about what words to use and how to answer me.

"Jackson, I know your heart was in the right place, but I want you to hear me out. I was in your shoes, remember? Once upon a time, about a hundred years ago, I was a young doctor with a young wife and a little boy at home waiting for me. My practice was never as busy as yours seems to be, but I had to learn how to keep my priorities straight. So, let's talk and figure out if we can come up with a solution so you aren't working so damn hard all the time and you can have a better balance between work and being with your family. Sound good?"

"Thanks, Dad. Things weren't so hard when I started my practice, but the town is growing, and I am the only family practitioner in Lake Harmony. As more people moved into town, more people needed a doctor. It has gotten to be a lot, honestly. I know I'm burning the candle at both ends, but I just figured that's what a husband does. We work hard to make sure that our family has anything and everything they could need. That is what you always did for Mom and me. Maybe I am a bit old fashioned and my way of thinking is dated but that is just the way I think and feel. After Julia told me she was ready to ask me for a separation, I started reaching out to a few doctors from my residency days that I know who may be interested in becoming a partner. I need someone to help me take some of the patient load. I think that will give me the time back that I need to be with my family more."

Watching my dad, he starts to smile and says, "Good! I think you have a good plan of action to start with regarding work. As for the kids, be sure when you're home that you make a bigger attempt to connect. Just be present. Kids are forgiving, but they are also good at holding a grudge. Keep trying. That is the best advice I can give you, and never, ever take your family for granted."

Julia

I am with both of my sisters at the Day Spa, and we all signed up for massages and then a mani-pedi. Before heading to the spa, my sisters stormed up to my closet to pick out a dress for me to wear tonight. They decided on a red wrap dress they both pointed out will show off my assets and have Jackson on edge all night. It is in my favorite color, geranium red, with bell sleeves. Stella picked out some multi-color heels to wear with it and some bangle bracelets. She said my wrap dress needed some fun and whimsy, so I remember to be fun and flirty. *Good thinking, sis!*

The massage was amazing, and my bones feel like jelly. Now we're all sitting and relaxing, drinking champagne while getting our nails and toes painted. I picked out a red polish to match my dress. It makes me happy, and since this day is all about my happiness and a date with my sexy husband, I'm going to make sure I feel good and look even better.

Jackson is still out with Josie when I arrive home from the spa. I wonder what those two are up to since they were going out for lunch, and its already late afternoon. Since I seem to have the house to myself and time to relax, I might as well continue the pampering. I head upstairs to my bathroom and fill the tub. I see Stella's bath salts sitting there. I want to use those so I can let her know what I think. I grab my book and sink down into this heavenly water.

Oh my god, Stella! The bath salts she made me are incredible. The scent is so intense but not overly done. She may finally be on to something she can do because I need more of these salts. I would use these salts every time I soak! *I need her to make me more. A lot more.*

I soak and read my book in the tub. I've added hot water about three times. I must be a prune by now. I hear soft knocking at the door and see Jackson poke his head around the door, smiling.

"Hi, are you enjoying yourself in this lovely field of lavender?"

"Yes, I am. Oh my god! Stella made these bath salts with infused lavender, and I haven't wanted to get out. They are heavenly."

With laughter in his eyes, he says, "I thought I better come up here and make sure you haven't fallen asleep because you've been up here for at least an hour since I got home with Josie."

I start to get up, and he puts his hand up. "Honey, stay. If you're getting some time in to take care of yourself, then stay put and relax. It smells amazing. The minute I came into our bedroom, it was like standing in the middle of a lavender field. How was the spa day with your sisters?"

I smile, adding, "Oh, it was perfect honey. It was so nice to spend those hours with them. Ellen is always working when I see her at her shop, and Stella was relaxed and full of fun today. I need to tell her that her bath salts are amazing. I may have to do this every day!"

"You should! I'll go down and make sure the kids have their things for your parents. What are they doing tonight?"

"Dad and Daniel are going to the new Stephen King movie, and Mom and Josie are doing their own 'girl' thing. They didn't want to go to a scary movie."

"Gotcha. Okay, you enjoy yourself. We have about two hours before we need to head out for dinner. Take your time."

I watch him as he walks over, leans down to give me a kiss, and lets his hand skim my breast. His eyes have that look that tells me the last thing he wants to do is leave. He straightens back up, winks, and walks out, shutting the door as he leaves.

A trip to the spa, a romantic date with my husband, and the house to ourselves tonight is the best end to this day. I have the perfect sexy lingerie to wear under that red wrap dress. I am going to give him a little surprise when he takes the time to unwrap me after dinner.

Another knock and a quiet, "Mom?" from Josie.

"Come on in, Josie."

I see her slowly open the door and peek in, "Hi, Mom. Dad wanted me to tell you that you can take your time getting ready. Daniel is going to drive us over to Gram's house. I have all my overnight stuff packed."

"Have a great time tonight and give them both a kiss from me. I will see you in the morning. Love you!"

"Love you, too!"

After a few more minutes, I figure it's time to get out of the tub and get dressed. If the kids are going to Mom and Dad's house now, we can get ready and head out to have a drink at the bar before dinner.

I get out of the tub and dry off before I apply some body lotion. I take time to dry and curl my long hair and put a little extra effort into getting ready tonight. Now, I get to put on the new lace bra set I bought at the boutique and wrap the dress around me. I love this dress, and the way it wraps around my body yet shows a little cleavage, which will surely have Jackson restless all night. Smiling, I put on the jewelry and shoes and head down to look for him.

I see him sitting in the family room watching something on the television. This man still brings a flutter to my belly. He is one good-looking man, and I love that he is mine. I say to him from the doorway, "Honey, since the kids are already out for their night with my parents, I thought we could get ready to go and maybe head out a little earlier and grab a drink at the bar before dinner." I watch as my husband turns toward me and see when his eyes go wide. His smile stretches across his face as his eyes devour me from top to bottom.

Standing, he walks over towards me with a determined attack. "Jules, you take my breath away. You are gorgeous. Are you trying to kill me all through dinner? I don't know if I'll be able to keep my hands off you. Wow!"

"I am glad you like what you see, honey, but go on and get ready and put that thought on hold until after you wine and dine me. I will straighten and lock up down here while I wait for you." I smile and wink at my husband. I watch him as he stands up, marches over to me, and grabs me around the waist. He kisses me and trails the kisses to my throat. With a whisper in my ear, I hear *I love you*, and then a nip to my earlobe. He backs away with a smile, smacks me on the butt, and winks before turning and quickly heading upstairs.

We park the car, and Jackson walks around to my door to help me out. He grabs my hand and gives me a small kiss, then with his hand on my lower back, he guides me into the restaurant. We have thirty minutes or so until our table is ready, so we tell the hostess we will be in the bar area.

Jackson orders a glass of white wine for me and a bourbon old-fashioned for himself. Once we have our drinks, he turns to me for a toast, "To us and never forgetting what is important. I love you, Jules." We clink our glasses, and he gives me a kiss.

Our dinner arrives at our secluded table and looks delicious. I ordered the lobster tail and he ordered a sirloin steak. He leans over and says, "How about a bite for a bite?" lifting his fork to my mouth.

"Mmm...that is so good. Oh god, that steak just melts in your mouth. Here, now try a bite of the lobster." I lift a piece of butter-dipped lobster to his mouth.

"That's delicious, too. Thank you for sharing, honey."

We finish our dinners and decide to share a dessert of crème brulée with fresh berries and cognac. Neither of us has room, but it looked too good to pass on, so sharing made sense.

Looking at Jackson and how handsome he is makes me smile. I am so lucky to call this man my husband. This evening was just what we needed. We shouldn't need a special occasion to have date nights like this together. That is something that we need to promise each other moving forward.

Standing, he grabs my hand. "Jules let's move back into the bar area and grab a spot. The live music is great tonight, and I want to get you in my arms for a couple of dances."

He takes my hand, and then escorts me into the bar with his hand low on my back. We find a high-top table close enough to the dancing but far enough to talk still. He pulls my chair out and helps me into my seat.

I watch my husband slide his chair closer to mine. Although the table isn't that large, he moves closer to me. As he sits, he leans forward and gives me a kiss on the lips and holds my hand. "Let's promise each other right now that we take the time to do this more often and not just for special occasions. Spending time with my beautiful wife is the perfect reason, and I'm sorry we haven't done it more, but we will."

"I had that same thought when we were finishing dinner. Yes, I promise that we will do this more often. As much as I love time with the kids, we need to make time for just us."

A slow song begins to play, and my husband stands up and holds his hand out to me. "Can I have this dance with my beautiful wife?"

Smiling, I reach out to take his hand, and he glides me into his arms and onto the dance floor. The song playing is one of our favorites by Eric Clapton, 'Wonderful Tonight'. As we dance in each other's arms, Jackson softly sings along, whispering the lyrics into my ear. He sings to me about feeling wonderful and how much he loves me. As his words and breath reach my ear, I begin to melt into my husband and just allow the moment and his words to carry me away.

After a few more slow dances, he pulls me close and whispers into my ear, "Honey, if I don't get you home right now, I'm going to slowly drag my hands up your thighs and under your dress on this dance floor."

Looking up into my husband's eyes, I see that look he could devour me. I say breathlessly, "Let's hurry home. So, you can do just that."

$$\infty \infty \infty$$

We make our way into the house, and I grab his hand and walk straight up to our room. I stop in front of the bed and turn to him. "I had the most romantic evening with you tonight. Now, I need you, Jackson. I need you to make me feel good. Please, Jackson, make love to me."

He pulls me into my chest, tips my head up, and glides his

thumb over my lower lip, leaning forward and nipping it with his teeth. "I'm going to love you tonight with my mouth and hands, and then I'll slide into you and make love to you all night long. I am not going to leave anything untouched tonight."

He steps back and sinks to his knees. He gently lifts my foot and removes my stiletto, then kisses my arch and gently lowers my foot. Then he repeats the motions with my other foot. Moving his hands up my thighs, he gently runs his hands over my hips and stands.

"Let's see what we have under here. You know how much I have always enjoyed unwrapping you." He grabs the tie around my waist to the dress and very slowly starts to pull the tie loose. My dress opens, and I hear him inhale and look at the lace I'm wearing under my dress.

"Mmm...what a nice surprise for me." He looks into my eyes, and I see they have a hunger and need for me in them. He drags his hands up the front of my body, and when he gets to my shoulders, he pushes the dress off my arms, and it pools around my feet. I am standing there only in my lace bra and panties.

Slowly, his strong hands move up my arms, down my body, and over my breasts. He slowly runs his thumb over my nipple and pinches, then moves to the other side and repeats the motion and pinch. My nipples harden, and I feel the pinch all the way to my center as it starts to build my need for him. His hand slowly moves down to my thigh and grazes my inner thigh, moving towards my center. With a slow rhythm, he swipes his finger over my center and stills.

"I can feel how wet you are through your panties." He moves his hand down and slowly slides under my panties, his finger runs once over my slit, and I groan, and my head falls back. "More. Please, now." He begins working a finger in and out of me, then adding a second. My need is building, and I shut all the noise in my head out except for this amazing feeling that is building. His other hand comes up, and his fingers twist into my hair as his mouth comes down on me, and he ravages my tongue with his own need. I am so close; my inner walls are starting to spasm.

I hear Jackson. "Come for me. Now!" as he presses against my clit with his thumb, and I explode.

My orgasm hits me so hard that he holds me up while I completely come undone. I moan his name over and over as he continues to work his fingers in and out of me pulling every spasm from me. He slowly straightens and looks in my eyes with a smile. "Beautiful."

After I catch my breath, I say, "You have too many clothes on, and here I am in only my panties."

"Then take my clothes off. I need to be inside you."

Smiling, I unbutton his shirt, and, with each button, I kiss his chest, working my way down. I watch his eyes and see that with each soft touch and kiss of his chest, his eyes become darker. I slowly push his shirt off his shoulders and let it fall to the floor. I remove his belt and then move to his zipper. As I pull the zipper down, I feel his hardness against my hand. I cup his penis through his boxers and lightly squeeze. I watch his eyes close as he groans.

Pushing his pants down and off with his boxers, I put my fingers around him and begin to slide my hand up and down him. As I get to the base, I squeeze and watch him grow even harder in my hand. I use the pre-cum, move my thumb over the tip, and continue to pump him. I drop down to my knees and look up at him as I roll my tongue around the tip of his penis and then lick from base to tip. His eyes close, and I watch him make fists at his sides. I continue to suck and lick, moving my hand to his balls and lightly squeezing. He loudly groans my name as I continue to move up and down, sucking and squeezing, taking him into the back of my throat. I know he is close, but he grabs me under the arms and pulls me up.

"My turn. As much as I want to watch you swallow all of me, I need to be inside you more. If I knew what was waiting for me under this dress, I would have never had dessert at the restaurant but would have come home and feasted on you instead."

His eyes and then his fingers and mouth are moving all over me. He moves to the clasp on my bra, opens it, and pushes the straps from my shoulders. It falls to the floor with the rest of our clothes. I am standing there in only my panties.

"Jules, get on the bed."

I move to the bed, lay down with my head on the pillows, and reach out for my husband. He moves closer to the bed, puts his thumbs into the sides of my panties, and slowly pulls them off. I let my knees fall to the side and watch him as he looks at me. He moves toward the bed and comes between my legs on the bed.

"I love you so much." He then kisses each of my eyelids and moves to my mouth. "I want to watch you as I fill you. I want to watch your eyes as we connect with nothing between us."

He enters me in one thrust, and I moan out his name as he fills me completely. He begins to move, takes both of my hands, and interlocks our hands together on each side of my head. He kisses me with such passion and emotion that I can feel the love pouring out of him. I feel a tear slide down my cheek because I am so overwhelmed at this moment. He kisses it away, and, with all the love in his eyes, he tells me that he loves me again and always will.

"Honey, I need more. Harder. Please."

He grabs my hips and rotates me, pulling my leg over his hip to get a better angle. I feel him even deeper now as he pushes harder and faster into me. He takes his thumb and presses on my clit, and I explode. The orgasm takes me over from head to toes, and nothing else matters but this overwhelming sensation that takes my breath away. I think I screamed his name but at this point I can't focus on anything as I feel another orgasm building in my center. He keeps driving into me harder and harder until I start to spasm, and this orgasm takes him over with me.

We lie there in bed, both trying to catch our breath. He pulls the covers up over us and then pulls me into his chest. The last thing I remember is putting my hand on his chest and telling him *I love you* before falling into a deep sleep.

Chapter Twenty-Four

Julia

I'm meeting with the girls at Harmonious Bites to show them the selfies we took last night and talk about last night's date. I had the hostess take our picture at our table, and we sent it to everyone this morning while snuggling in bed.

I walk into the shop and see Ellen already at our usual table with Sam waving me back. Right behind me, Bree walks in, so I wait with her as she puts her order in at the counter. She puts her hand around my arm, and we head back toward our table.

"So, you look all smiley this morning, Mrs. Harte." She whispers in my ear with a giggle. "I expect to hear lots of juicy love bits from you this morning."

I don't have to answer as I feel my face heat with my blush. Then I look up to see Hill and Griffin walking in, placing their order and rushing back.

"Hey, gorgeous," Griffin says with a wink. "You know I had to join the ladies this morning when Hill said this was the 'tell all' coffee hour! Just because I enjoy a good hunky man doesn't mean I don't want to hear all about your sexy night, darling. Plus, you have one helluva hunky man."

"Oh my god, you guys, fine." I take a deep breath and exhale with the biggest smile possible. "It was absolutely amazing and... delicious, and the dinner was good too."

They all burst out laughing, and Griffin gives me a high-five and shouts, "YES, girl- you got some sexy times!"

We talk about the date with dinner and dancing and the few details I am willing to share from after we got home. We are all catching up and sharing how things are going when Griffin jumps up and yells, "I GOT IT! I got date four!!!!"

Not only has our table stopped talking to stare at him but so has the entire shop full of patrons getting their coffee fix on this Sunday morning.

"Shh, Griffin, sit down, please," I say with wide but amused eyes.

Hill leans over to her goofy assistant. "Why should you get to assign a date, Griff? What are you thinking because sometimes you have great outside-the-box ideas?"

"Hill, your chef friend is coming into town this week to look at a new restaurant spot in the city, remember. He's coming here to see you for a few days. So, what about a private cooking class with him for Jules and Jackson in your kitchen."

"Damn, that is a great idea. Hold, please."

I watch as Hill grabs her phone and starts punching in a text to someone. Almost immediately, she gets a return text, smiles, and looks at me.

"What's your favorite Italian dish you and Jackson like to eat?"

"I like anything, but Jackson loves any kind of pasta and vodka sauce. Why?"

"HOLD, Please."

I watch as Hillary is texting back and forth with someone and whispering in Griffin's ear. They are having a total whisper conversation in front of all of us, and then they both stop, turn, and smile at us.

"Jules, you and Jackson have a private cooking class with Anthony at my work kitchen on Wednesday night. He will help you make homemade pasta and even bring the wine to pair it with. Date four scheduled. Good job, Griffin!"

I head home to see how Josie and Daniels' night was with my parents. I am walking into the kitchen, and my phone starts buzzing in my purse. Pulling it out, I see a text chain going so I open it up.

Hill: Date 4 scheduled courtesy of Griffin
Hill: What? Private cooking lesson for two with Chef Anthony
Hill: When? Wed @ 6:30pm in my work kitchen
Julia: Thank you! That sounds amazing
Bree: Aww, just like Lady and the Tramp
Rob: Tramp *laughing emoji* PERFECT
Jackson: Seriously Rob? Don't say that about your sister
Rob: Um, Jackson...LADY and the tramp means you are the tramp
Cooper: Idiots
Garrett: Cool! make extra for me pls
Sam: I think this means we have pasta night soon at their place since they are getting lessons from chef
Ellen: ^^^what she said
Scott: Ditto^^^
Stella: So romantic *heart eye emoji*

Laughing, I walk into the family room and see Josie and Daniel. "Hey guys, how was your night?"

Daniel smiles. "What's so funny?"

"Oh, just reading the group text about our fourth date this week. Dad and I are having a cooking lesson with a chef."

"Hey, Mom, I was going to ask you about that. You are supposed to go on five dates with dad, right? These dates are supposed to make dad see what he's been missing, right?"

I laugh at my son and ask, "Who told you that?"

"Uncle Rob said that since Dad is never around, everyone is telling you guys what the dates will be, and that's supposed to get him to realize what he's missing."

I see that Rob, as usual, has put his own spin on things. I look at my kids and decide to clarify a little bit for their sake and ours. "I know you both have felt upset and maybe even a little angry because Dad has been so busy. Work seems to take him away from the things we do as a family. Let's talk about this for a minute. I went to talk to someone to figure out how to help me work on some things and to help Dad understand that he needed to be around more. You know what they always say, 'It takes two to make a problem and two to fix it.' Your dad and I love each other very much, and you are his world. So, together we are trying to make a point of spending time together to, as you said, 'show him what he's missing' but also to help us reconnect and remind us how much we love each other. Do you understand that?"

Both kids say yes, and then Daniel looks at his sister and whispers in her ear. She nods at him, then smiles big, and Daniel says, "Mom, Josie, and I want to plan your last date. Date five."

"That works for m. Go ahead. I can't wait to see what you both come up with."

"We can work on it now and let you and Dad know the plan at dinner."

I watch my kids from the kitchen as I grab a glass of water and head to the porch. After a few minutes, I decide to grab my gardening gloves and work on my roses out in the yard. I yell for Duke to come out and keep me company while I work.

After a little while, I hear the door open and close and look up to see my husband on the stairs of the porch, leaning against the railing, smiling. "Hey honey, what are you up to?"

He heads down into the grass towards me. Duke goes running up to him for head scratches and then comes back trailing Jackson.

"I don't want to interrupt you while you're enjoying your garden, but do you know what the kids are up to? I walked into the family room where they're talking and have notes all around them, and they stopped immediately and told me to please leave. They look like they are about to cause some mischief."

I stand up and take off my gardening gloves and go up on my toes to kiss my husband, "Ah yes, they are doing exactly that, I think." Laughing, I tell him, "Daniel and Josie are planning our last date. Date five."

"I don't know if I should be happy or terrified. Daniel has been angry with me these last couple of months. I don't want to do anything that will upset him and make him angrier. I also don't know if I trust him not to make me do something ridiculous."

"Honey, it will be fine. I mean, Hill made us do that Goodwill Challenge, and it was a fun night. Let's not worry yet. They said they'll share the date plan with us at dinner. I am kind of glad that they want to be part of it. Let's just go with whatever they cook up, okay?"

"Fine. Are you done working in your roses to come sit and snuggle with me on the porch swing?"

"I'm never too busy for you—let me clean up quickly."

Snuggling and swinging slowly on the porch swing together, we talk about last night's date and, again, how we're not going to wait for a specific reason to have a romantic night together. It was perfect from start to finish.

"So, can you tell me any more details about what this cooking date is about? I saw that this was Griffin's idea. Is that right?"

"Yep, he crashed coffee with the girls because he was helping Hill clean up from last night's catering job. He remembered that Hill's friend, Anthony, the chef with those fancy Italian restaurants, is coming to Lake Harmony this weekend to catch up with her. So, Hill texted him to see if he would do a private lesson for the two of us at her kitchen at the shop, and he agreed. So, we're doing that on Wednesday, and then the kids want to plan our last date on the weekend."

"Now I understand Rob's comment about Lady and the Tramp."

Laughing, I kiss him and snuggle in closer. "Love you."

"Love you more. That sounds fun. I'm looking forward to it. Do you have any idea what we're learning to cook?"

"I may have mentioned that you love pasta and vodka sauce."

"Oh, now I'm *very* excited."

We stay like that and snuggle closer while the kids plan their date for us. It's days like this that we haven't seemed to have for a long time. The kids are at home, doing something together. Jackson and I are watching our kids and having time just to be still and focus on being a family.

"Honey, maybe we can have a game night with the kids after dinner."

He must be thinking about how nice it is to have a normal family day too. "I'd like that. Let's skip family dinner at Mom's and just order a pizza or Chinese for dinner. Then we can ask the kids to pick a game."

∞∞∞

Sitting around the dinner table eating pizza and Caesar salad, everyone is chatting, and it just feels...normal. *How long has it been since we've done this?*

Daniel looks over at Josie, and she nods at him. "Josie and I have planned your date five. On Saturday, the town is having a 'Movie in the Park' night as a fundraiser to fix the fountain and flowers in the park that were damaged from whoever wrecked it with dye. We saw the Facebook post on Harmony Hears that they're doing a concession stand before selling popcorn. We signed you both up today with Miss Gertie to work the booth for an hour before the movie. The date is working concessions and watching the movie together, but we decided that your date includes us. We're watching the movie as a family, so it turned into family date night. That's okay, right? That still counts as your date?" Daniel asks, almost nervously.

The kids sit there holding their breath after telling us what the date will be. They worked together all day to plan this for their father and me, and it's perfect. I don't answer right away, but Jackson does.

"That is awesome! I didn't see that they were doing a movie in the park at night. Do you know what they're showing? I assume it's family-friendly, right?"

Josie grins big and shouts, "THE GOONIES!" which happens to be one of our family favorites.

"Wow, that couldn't be more perfect. The date and the movie," Jackson answers.

Well done, kiddos, well done. "Are there any more posts on Harmony Hears that we missed?"

Daniel says, "Just something about The Yellow Lady being sold and Miss Gertie is all crazy about who it could be."

I gasp and look at my husband. "I didn't even know she was on the market. Where is the Phillips Family going?"
"I think they're downsizing and looking to move to a warmer climate closer to their grandkids. I'm looking forward to the movie and our family date. Let's hope the weather holds out and the entire town doesn't want to eat popcorn."

I grab my phone and pull up Facebook. I want to look for that post. I can't believe the house was sold. I let out a large sigh and turn my phone toward Jackson. "Look. I love that house. I hope whoever bought it loves it the right way."

The Yellow Lady - SOLD

Rumor has it our pride and joy, The Yellow Lady, that looks out at Lake Harmony on the bluff has been sold. The current owners, Mr. and Mrs. Phillips, seem to have sold the beautiful old Victorian home without ever putting her on the market. Who is the scoundrel that has stolen her out from under the town's nose? She is a grand lady and needs to be respected and so her new owner better understand she is meant to stay that way, or else there will be many unruly residents here.

Chapter Twenty-Five

Jackson

It's Monday morning, and I have a smile on my face. I had an amazing weekend with my family. A very romantic and passionate night with my wife followed by an awesome day and night at home with my family. My kids are not angry with me today, and things seem to be shaping up great. My phone rings and I look down with a smile and chuckle, answering, "Dr. Harte."

"Good morning, Dr. Harte. This is Dr. Noah Roark. I believe you called and left me a message that your life is in ruins, and you need my ass to come bail you out?"

I burst out with a loud and deep laugh. "Oh my god, Noah, that was just what I needed from you. Man, how are you and, yes, let's talk. How would you feel about being part of an amazing small-town practice and enjoying the 'burbs?'"

"Hey man, I may very well be interested in just that scenario. I have some time I need to take off this week. Let's look at our calendar and see what works. I could be very interested in what you have to offer."

"Noah, I'm so glad to hear that. Can you meet me somewhere for dinner this week? I'm free all but Wednesday. I'd like to talk somewhere we won't be overheard or interrupted. Julia isn't aware I'm looking for a partner. The practice is just getting too big for a one-person show. If you are seriously considering this, I would be really happy to talk in person."

"Jackson, I am. Man, I need a change too, and the sooner, the better. I'd have to give my current partners time to work me off the schedule and notify patients, but I need to get out of the city. As big as Chicago is, it is still too small for my liking. I need to open myself up to new surroundings and not be running in the same friend group as my ex-wife and her new boyfriend. We split amicably, but she's now dating a mutual friend of ours, and, well, the rest of our friend group is having a tough time staying neutral. I think for my sake, I need to find something new."

"Noah, I'm really sorry to hear that. I didn't know Stacy well, but I always liked her. I am sorry that it didn't work out for you."

"Being a busy doctor and taking on cases that had me working around the clock didn't bode well for my marriage. The final straw was when she decided having children with a doctor like me would be like being a single parent. She admitted to me she was unhappy and wanted a different life. I couldn't blame her, and we grew apart. We became like roommates, not spouses. But enough about me. How are you doing? How are Julia and the kids?"

With a big sigh, I answer, "I'm looking for a partner, so I don't lose my family. Does that answer your question?"

"Shit! I'm sorry to hear that, Jackson."

"Things are a little better now. Jules finally talked to me, and honestly, I was a bit selfish and blind to the whole problem. I got lost in the process of providing for my family and giving them everything they could want or need, except I forgot that they wanted me to be part of it. Now we're all working on it. For better or worse, it feels like the whole town is secretly involved."

"I'm almost afraid to ask, but as long as you are both willing to fight for your marriage, there is still hope. You'll figure it out. I've never seen two people more in love than you and Julia. Okay, how does Thursday night sound?"

"Like the perfect time. I will let Jules know I have a business dinner. At least it won't be a surprise."

After hanging up the phone with Noah I was finally feeling like I was making progress with my side of making changes for my family. Noah would make a great partner, and his specialties would balance nicely with mine. It could even bring in some new patients with the growth of the town. Finally, things were looking up on my to-do list.

Chapter Twenty-Six

Julia

Week four and my appointment with Dr. Rose was today. When I sit here and think about how I was feeling just a month ago, I'm so glad my life seems to be moving in the right direction. My marriage seems to be getting back on track, and my family is happy and whole again. The only thing that hasn't changed is me: How I feel, what I need to make myself feel whole again. *Ugh, why is this so hard? I can fix everything and everyone else.* Dr. Rose and I put the focus on me this session. She said the bottom line is that I still need to find a way to stop feeling guilty for needing something for myself and allow myself the time to rediscover what my purpose is and what will give me fulfillment and purpose.

Walking out of the office, I feel motivated to try and ready to figure out this business idea. By the time I'd reached my car, I'd decided to head over to Mom's. Maybe she can brainstorm with me and figure out what direction I should take. As I walk up to the front door, it opens, and there's my mom with a smile.

"Julia, I wasn't expecting you, but I'm always happy to see my beautiful daughter."

"Thanks, Mom, I just had my therapy appointment, and I hoped you were home. Do you have time for a cup of coffee?"

"That I do, and I may even have some warm lemon bars."

We walk into Mom's bright kitchen. I love the open windows all along the back wall of the kitchen and the kitchen nook Dad built for her. She points at me to sit down, brings a plate with lemon bars over to the table, and then grabs two cups of coffee. "These look great. I love when they're still warm and gooey from the oven."

"Help yourself and eat as much as you want." She sits quietly and doesn't say more until, "Now, talk to me, honey. You look like you are a little lost today."

"I think I am, at least a little bit. I just left Dr. Rose, and we talked about the dates Jackson and I have gone on and how things are going between us. Things are good, great even. We have had the chance to reconnect over the last couple weeks with these dates. Last weekend, the date you and Dad planned, it was perfect. We both realized that if our relationship is strained, everything else is off balance too. My biggest struggle is ME, Mom. I still feel like I have no self-worth or purpose. Who am I other than a mom, wife, daughter, friend? I need more. I love all those things, but I still have this void, a missing purpose. Is that selfish? I just feel so guilty that my life isn't enough to make me happy. I have such an amazing family, and I couldn't ask for better friends who would do anything for me. What else do I need to do to find myself, to feel whole?"

Grabbing my hand and holding it between her hands, she says, "No, Julia, that is not selfish. You are remarkable in all those titles you hold, but I understand. You had big dreams of having your own business after college, and then you got busy helping Dad with how quickly the business was growing, and then you started building your beautiful family. There is nothing wrong with wanting more now that your children are growing up and you have time to put toward something that fulfills you. Where are you with thinking about that?"

"Jackson and I have talked about it a lot lately. He is being so supportive and told me he will support any decision I make. As a team, we made his dreams come true, and now he has his practice. My dreams just got lost or buried along the way. I don't regret putting my focus on my family and his practice, but he wants me to think about opening my own business now. Something that makes me happy and brings me joy."

"That does sound like a good idea, and I am happy to hear

that he is supporting you with whatever you decide."

"Yeah, the problem is I have no idea what that would be." Discouraged, I tilt my head to her shoulder. Mom shifts closer and starts rubbing my back.

"Honey, it will be okay, I promise. You just need to make yourself a priority and think about what makes you happy and see if you can build off that. No one can tell you what to do or what will make you feel happy and whole. Only listening to your heart will help you make that connection."

After a few minutes, I lift my head up and wipe my tears. "Mom, what do I do? I don't even know how to put myself first?" "Oh, honey, that is because you are a caregiver. I want you to understand, though, that it isn't selfish of you to need something for yourself. Why don't we talk about what you enjoy doing and see if you can put some thoughts together and then focus on those."

I pull out my journal from my purse and show Mom the list I've already made:

What makes you happy?

What do you enjoy doing that you could make into a business?

> *organizing parties and events*
> *working in the garden and flower beds*
> *being with friends and family*
> *movies/music/dancing*

Mom looks at what I wrote down. "You definitely went into specific areas here, and you do excel at all of them: Organizing events, being with people, entertainment, and gardening. There are a lot of things you can do with this."

"Gardening is what Sam and Paul have with the garden center and his landscape architecture work. I can't copy that and work against them. Working with them kind of defeats the purpose of my own business."

"Makes sense, and that could end up being seasonal in the

Midwest. You also have event and party planning. I agree that you are good at that and do it so effortlessly, Julia. Maybe that is the direction that you should go?"

"I could, but how much of a need is there for that, and will it overshadow what the country club does or even Hillary's catering business."

"At least this conversation has you starting to look at the possibilities, and maybe you can combine them all. What about having your own event venue? Or something similar? The only other venue for things around Lake Harmony is the Golf and Country Club. Maybe something on a smaller scale, more personal?"

Mom may have a great idea here and it is something that appeals to me. *Hmm, is this something that I could do?* I love creating unique moments for people, and this may be something to put my focus on. Smiling, I lean over and hug Mom. "I think you finally sparked my brain into gear, Mom. Maybe if I look at it all creatively, I can combine the things I enjoy, and I may be able to overlap and work with my best friends."

As I head home in the car, my mind is going crazy with a lot of possibilities. One of my favorite songs comes on the radio, "Landslide" by Stevie Nicks, and, like always, I sing along. Singing about changes and whether she can handle those changes. This song could be about my life and this moment I'm stuck in.

As I finish singing the chorus, I realize that one of my favorite songs fits what I'm going through right now. *I hear you, Universe. Do I take a chance on myself and pursue a dream at this stage in my life? If I'm too afraid to make those changes, will I forever feel this lack of self-worth and continue to have regrets about where my professional life never went?*

Tonight, is our date with Chef Anthony, and I am so excited. So far, Jackson is on schedule and there's no pending emergency in sight, so that is promising. I want to dress up and look cute for him, but not too fancy, since we're going to be working with pasta and vodka sauce. I decided on a pair of my skinny jeans and a cute top. I need to get ready so I can either make something for the kids or order them a pizza. As I get ready, I freshen my makeup, put my long hair up into a cute sexy twist knot, but I can't stop thinking about my conversation with Mom.

How can I combine all those things that I enjoy doing? Is having my own small event venue something that I would enjoy doing? But where is there something around here that would fit that purpose and not compete with what Lake Harmony already has? I need to talk to Jackson about this and see if he has some advice.

Jackson got home tonight without an issue, the kids wanted pizza, and it's been delivered, and now the both of us are heading to Hillary's shop for our private cooking lesson with Chef Anthony. We are both looking forward to the evening and getting hungrier by the minute. As we park and head into Hillary's shop, *A Matter of Taste*, I see Griffin standing behind the counter with a big grin on his face.

"Welcome to your romantic evening with Chef Anthony. Please join me in the kitchen," Griffin says with a dramatic bow and big hand gesture. "Guests first."

Before Griffin heads back up front, he leans into us and says, "Just an FYI, I will be upfront so when your wonderful evening ends, I can come back and clean up, but just remember, no sexy times in the kitchen once Chef leaves. That is our number one rule. Well, Hillary's rule, so don't break it. We don't want to witness her veins popping out of her head and neck while she yells at us because you two couldn't keep your naked bits covered."

Jackson shakes his head, and we both laugh. "No worries, Griff, we'll keep our naked bits off the kitchen counters."

"One more thing, I got you both aprons to wear so you don't mess up your clothes. Here's one for you, Jackson."

I watch Jackson put the apron on and bust out laughing. His apron has 'Not only sexy but can cook too,' which Griffin explains he bought especially for my husband. Jackson knows Griffin loves to flirt with him, so he is a good sport and tells Griffin he picked the right one. Then he hands me my apron, and it says, 'kiss the cook.'

Jackson reaches over, grabs me, and puts a big kiss on my lips. "What? Just following directions."
Chef Anthony has met us before, so we all say hello and talk about how his business is growing and the new space he's in town for to look at an expansion. We talk about what's on the menu and go to the sink to wash up.

"I hear that Jackson loves vodka sauce, so we're going to make some homemade pappardelle pasta with vodka sauce. Everything we need is on the counter in front of us, so let's begin."

We start with the pasta and learn how to make it from scratch. I have never used a pasta maker since I usually just buy the pasta already made from the store. We follow directions on how to make the pasta, and each has a little well of flour and egg in front of us, mixing and slowly creaming the eggs into the flour on the table using our hands. Once the dough is made and covered, we let it sit and rest. At this point, we move over to the sauce.

Chef Anthony says, "We're going to make homemade vodka sauce since that is your favorite, Jackson. In front of you, we have some delicious Italian peeled tomatoes and all the ingredients you need to make the sauce. While we wait for the pasta to rest and the gluten to do its magic, we can start putting the sauce together. Now grab the onions and pancetta. We need to slice the pancetta into strips and dice the onions. Jackson, you can start with that while Julia crushes the tomatoes gently."

Jackson starts working on those two items while I take the tomatoes and slowly crush them after adding salt and pepper to bring the flavors out. Once we have that prepared, we work together to heat the onions and pancetta up in the pan. The pancetta will become crispy and add some flavor to our sauce, along with the onions that are slowly cooking down. The smell in the kitchen is heavenly. I glance at my husband, who is slowly stirring the deliciousness that is cooking in the pan. He looks up at me and winks. Once that's ready, we add the vodka to the pan, cooking it slowly to allow the alcohol to evaporate but leaving the flavor in the pan. When that is complete, we add the tomatoes to simmer and reduce on low heat, so we have time to go back to the pasta.

"Oh my god, Anthony, this smells delicious. I can't wait to eat it."

Jackson leans into me and whispers, "I can't wait to eat you, baby."

"Behave, Mister."

Since the sauce is reducing, we now learn how to prepare homemade pasta. We watch Chef Anthony as he shows us how to work the pasta machine. He advises us that Pappardelle needs to get to setting number six for the right consistency and thickness. Jackson and I take turns working the pasta through the machine and watch it slowly stretch out and thin down to the thickness it needs to be. We gently fold it and cut the finished dough into strips to be added to the boiling pot. We have the pasta finished, so we move back to the reducing sauce. Now that the tomato sauce has reduced, and fresh basil has been added, we can slowly add the heavy cream to the red sauce to create a creamy texture to the vodka sauce. Now combined and finished, we leave the sauce on a low simmer to keep it warm and begin to finish the pasta. We heat the salted water and slowly add the homemade noodles. They need to cook for about five to six minutes, and then we can strain them and add the noodles directly to the sauce.

While the pasta is finishing, Chef Anthony walks toward us, "You guys did a great job, and it was fun catching up while we cooked. I can't believe you've never made pasta from scratch before. You both looked like pros to me. Great teamwork putting this dinner together."

The pasta is done, added to the sauce, and coated generously with pecorino cheese—we're about to take our first bite.

Chef Anthony comes towards us with a bottle of wine in his hand, smiling. "This is my gift to you. I love showing friends how to prepare a meal from scratch, and to finish off this delicious dinner, I want to pour you each a glass of the wine I pair with this dish in the restaurant. This is a Sauvignon Blanc with high acidity and a citrus quality that contrasts nicely with the richness of the dish." He pours us each a glass and then says goodbye and thanks us for a great evening.

I turn toward my husband and raise my wine glass, "To us and never forgetting what matters." He clinks his glass to mine, and then we each take a sip and dig into our meal.

The food is amazing, and we both can't seem to stop long enough to talk to each other. I take a moment to enjoy another sip of wine and turn to Jackson. "Honey, I had my appointment today with Dr. Rose, and it was good, but I'm still unsettled about my personal changes. I even stopped by my mom's after my appointment because I felt a little lost and not sure how to move forward. We talked about how I was feeling and what steps to take next. She was great about hearing my ideas and helping me see if there was a connection to finding some sort of self-worth or purpose. We may have come up with something."

He smiles at me and leans forward to give me a gentle kiss. "Jules, that's great. I know you're not sure about having your own business, but have you given it some more thought or are you leaning in a different direction? Fill me in on what you've been thinking. You know I'm always here to listen."

"Mom and I talked about the thing I enjoy the most, which is organizing events and moments for people. I also love to work in the yard and make it pretty and a place to relax. She thought maybe having my own space, like a smaller venue, to host more intimate gatherings. What do you think?"

"I think that's a great idea, but the more important thing is what do YOU think?"

"I'm a little bit excited, but also very nervous. Do I want to take on that kind of pressure? Do I want to be the one responsible for making it work? Where in the world will I find the right location? Those are all things that I worry about, and it keeps me from saying yes to all of it."

"Honey, that isn't such a crazy idea. I honestly love it. We can talk about the details and see what we come up with if you want me to be part of building on your idea."

"Yes, I would love to have your input. Honey, we're a team, and if I do this, it will take time away from us, from our family time. Events and things are fun, but they usually happen on weekends. We're just starting to get on solid ground again. Do I really want to go and be the one that's always missing?"

"Before you say no and not investigate this further because of it taking you away from the family, let's sit down and list the pros and cons. Then we can try to simplify and look at it from all the angles."

"Let's finish this delicious dinner we made and then we can go home and sit down and talk about the next steps. First, let's take a quick selfie to send to our group for evidence of our date."

We finish our delicious dinner, give Griffin a to-go container with our pasta since he was the creator of this date, and head home. He refused our help to clean up, saying if we did it wrong, he would just have to do it again.

We hold hands in the car and head home to sit and enjoy

another glass of wine and talk about this event hosting idea.

Chapter Twenty-Seven

Jackson

Could it work in my favor that I went and bought the Yellow Lady without Jules's input?

We head into the house, both kids are home, and their pizza box is still open and on the counter with one slice left. Jules is pouring a glass of wine for each of us as I straighten the kitchen and clean up after our kids.

"Jules let's sit on the porch and talk about what you're thinking. Grab a pad of paper and something to write with, and we can brainstorm and see what we come up with."

I watch her take the wine onto the porch, let Duke out in the yard, and look in the kitchen junk drawer for paper and a pen. I finish wiping down the counter, turn off the light and follow her onto the porch. She's sitting on the porch swing, her feet up and tucked under her, and a pen in mouth as she stares at the paper.

"You look lost in thought. All okay?"

Smiling, I say, "Yes, I got as far as writing 'Events and Venue' on the top of the paper, and now I can't seem to get my thoughts straight."

"I'm here to talk it out with you, but before we do that, should we send our date evidence off to our nosey friends and family?" She nods, and since I took the picture, I send the photo off with a text.

Jackson: *image**image**image*
Jackson: Delicious dinner of pappardelle pasta in vodka sauce
Jackson: Griffin got the extra since it was his idea *thumbs up emoji*

Hillary: Glad it was a good date, Chef Anthony rocks!
Bree: So romantic *Emoji heart eyes*
Sam: Paul and I want a dinner date-you can cook
Ellen: Scott and I say ditto^^^
Stella: YUMMERS!
Rob: Where are my leftovers???
Garrett: In Griffin *laughing emoji*
Cooper: Looks great guys

"Now that we've sent the evidence, let's start with exactly what you talked about with your mom."

"We talked about it being a smaller, more intimate type of venue. Right now, all we have for hosting something is the Golf and Country Club or local restaurants. There isn't a middle ground anywhere within Lake Harmony. I was leaning towards a place that could host smaller-scale events and possibly with a yard or green space so that, if it were a lady's lunch or intimate wedding, we could do it outside. Of course, it would need a kitchen or prep space, but nothing to overlap Hill's business. Anyway, that is how far we got. What do you think?"

Taking a deep breath, *no time like the present*, I grab her hand. "So, honey, I may have done something crazy. But as crazy as it may seem, maybe it was fate. I don't want you to be mad, so hear me out." My wife's eyes are as big as dinner plates and I can tell she is holding her breath. I better tell her before she lets the worst-case scenario creep in. "I bought the Yellow Lady." Jules is still staring at me, not giving me any type of reaction.

After what feels like two hours, but more likely only a few seconds, she exhales and starts to talk.

"You WHAT?! What do you mean you bought the Yellow Lady? How...when...what? Jackson! What have you done?"

She gets up and starts pacing the porch, talking to herself under her breath and occasionally stopping and just staring at me. Her reaction is still mixed. I can't tell if she is angry or happy. Most likely, she's thinking I have lost my mind, but I couldn't let that house slip past us. It was always a dream that we would one day live there and grow old. *Could this be her intimate venue instead?*

"Honey, come here, please. Let me explain." I watch her come back over and sit down as she turns to face me.

"I saw that Gertie posted in Harmony Hears that the house was being sold. Then my patient that day just happened to be Mr. Phillips, the house owner. We talked about the house and how they were ready to sell and move closer to the kids and grandkids and that the house was just too much for the two of them. They also wanted to make sure that the house went to someone that would love it and treasure it as much as they did. I asked him what they wanted for it and, well, I thought about it and bought it for you."

"Jackson! Don't you think that this was something that we should have discussed before making such a large investment? What did you think we would do, move there? I love our home and the kids have so many friends in the neighborhood. I don't want to move. I love that house, but I really don't want to move."

She looks so sad, as if I'm about to ask her to uproot our family and move. Did I know what the hell I was going to do with this house when I offered to buy it from Mr. Phillips? No, but after talking with her, this may be the answer she hasn't quite seemed to put together for her venue yet.

"Honestly, honey, I couldn't let someone else buy it. We are doing fine financially, and we have investments, so if nothing else, we could have turned it and sold it to someone else. Jules, what about using the Yellow Lady and turning it into your venue?"

I just sit back and let her turn that thought around for a few minutes. I can almost see the wheels turning, she bites her lip while she is thinking and, slowly, she starts to write on the pad of paper in her lap. I just watch as her shock starts turning into what I think is excitement. I sit back and let her brainstorm, staying quiet so I don't interrupt her thoughts that seem to be coming more quickly. She continues to write, and I read along as she continues to jot down her thoughts.

So far, she has written:

Victorian House
Intimate space
Bedrooms/gathering rooms
Garden/outdoor space
Kitchen
Bluff/ isolated cove/beach-Private
Lake Harmony
Weddings/Birthdays
Square foot of house
Zoning/Permits
Parking lot?
Vendors

She stops, stares at me, and I see the biggest smile on her face. Her eyes have their sparkle back, and she leans over and gives me a kiss on the lips.

"Jackson, you may be the craziest husband around, but I love you. I love you for buying this house that we always dreamed about owning. I love you because you think I can have my own business, and you support me, no questions asked. I love you for believing I could use the Yellow Lady as my business. Thank you, Jackson, for loving me so much that you made an absolutely crazy decision without talking to me first, and I forgive you because I am so in love with you, and I love that house!"

"I would buy you the moon if I could, Jules. So, I see you have some ideas on that paper–want to talk about it?"

We talk late into the night about the house and if we can make it into an event venue. She wants to keep some rooms upstairs as bedrooms, so if she does have an intimate wedding or event, she can also host the guests overnight. There are things we need to check on with the village like zoning, permits, and if we can add parking to the area. Thankfully the house has its own long drive up the bluff and its own access road. As we talk, I see the sparkle in her eyes and the excitement of a business idea coming to life. My wife is glowing with excitement, and I am so glad to see the happiness back.

∞∞∞

Julia

As I lay in his arms and try to fall asleep, I am still so surprised and excited, so sleep is the furthest thing from happening right now. I can't believe my husband bought me the Yellow Lady. We talked for hours tonight after our fun dinner date with Chef Anthony. He let me brainstorm using the old Victorian home as a venue and then helped me with forming the next steps. It has so many possibilities that I am still lying here with thoughts running through my brain when dawn isn't too far away. I know I should try to fall asleep, or I will be a wreck all day from lack of sleep, but I can't seem to find my off button.

I feel his hand move on my back, "Honey, you haven't fallen asleep yet, have you?"

"I'm just so excited about having the house and planning to open a business. I can't seem to quiet down enough to sleep."

"Let me see if I can help with that."

He rolls me onto my back and stretches out above me. I can see him with the moonlight streaming in through the curtains. He focuses on my eyes and leans in to kiss me. His kiss is gentle and slow. He continues to kiss me in slow movements, his tongue dipping into my mouth and dancing with my own. He glides his hand down from my face to my neck, following with his mouth.

He slows and looks up at me, "Honey, focus on what you are feeling right now and what I am doing to you—not the house. Feel what I am doing to you and focus on how it feels. I want you to lose yourself in the feelings. Tell me what you want."

"Touch me, Jackson."

"Where? Tell me where you need me to touch you."

"Everywhere. With your hands and with your mouth. Make me stop thinking."

He continues kissing down my neck, moves to nibble my earlobe, and breathes quietly into my ear that he loves me. He moves from my neck to my shoulder and gives me a little bite. Leaning back, he sits up and drags my nightgown up and over my head and drops it to the floor. Now there is no barrier between his mouth and my body. He continues to move, kissing, sucking, and nipping his way down from my shoulder to my breast. He licks around my nipple, and I feel as it hardens into a tight bud, he sucks softly and then bites quickly, licking immediately after to ease the nip. From there, he moves to the other breast and repeats the same motion—lick, suck, nip, lick. The sensation is overwhelming my senses, and I feel my need building, and I need more.

"More, I need more. Now."

I can feel his smile against my skin, and then his hand moves lower, and I feel his finger glide softly across my center. "Is this what you need, honey?"

"Yes, more, please." I say as I slowly push him where I need him to be. I hate to beg, but that is exactly what I'm doing because I need to orgasm. I feel it building, and I just want that overflowing sense of relief that I know an orgasm will bring. He inserts his finger and then another, using the palm of his hand to move against my clit. I hear myself moaning and repeating his name. I need more still as I ride hard against his hand. He moves down me and adds his mouth, and as soon as he sucks my clit into his mouth, I explode. He continues to suck me until the last spasm, and I come down from another-worldly orgasm. He kisses my inner thigh and moves up my body, kissing all along the way. He reaches my face and kisses me, and I can taste myself on his tongue. Before I can even move, he pushes into me, and I say, "I love you."

"Love you to—now just feel, baby."

He begins to move in a slow and steady rhythm. He knows

exactly how to read my body and when I need more. He is in no hurry, but I still want more. He senses that my need is building again, and he grabs my hips and rotates me just a little, taking one of my legs and wrapping it around his waist. Now I can feel him even deeper, and it makes me feel even fuller. At this angle, he knows how to hit that sweet spot. The spot that he knows will take me up and over quickly. He continues to thrust in and out of me, getting faster and harder with each movement.

"Come for me. Now."

My orgasm hits hard and fast and it grabs him, and he falls over with me. We lay wrapped in each other until we both catch our breath. Pulling me into his side, he says, "Get some sleep, honey. Love you."

I yawn and answer, "Love you, too," and feel my surrender to sleep finally take over.

Chapter Twenty-Eight

Julia

It's Saturday morning, and as I relax and have coffee with the kids, we talk about the fundraiser and everything happening later today. I'm looking forward to the evening, and the excitement I see with the kids today makes it all worth it. We don't need to be at the park until our six o'clock shift at the popcorn stand. We need to work for an hour and then pass it to the next group. The kids bought all of us matching shirts with the Goonies movie logo on them. They said they want us in the mood and playing our part. Once we finish our shift, we'll join the kids in our lawn chairs and enjoy the movie together. Daniel and Josie claim they're in charge of getting dinner together for all of us to eat while we wait for the movie to start. I love watching them work together and be in cahoots with each other over something.

"So, guys, while Dad and I are handling popcorn duty, what are you going to do?"

"I was going to see if Sam and Paul need my help with the volunteer crew to replant the roses and fix up the fountain next week," Daniel says.

The fundraiser tonight is to help with the cost of the fountain repairs and damage to the landscape that was caused by someone a few weeks ago. I love that my children are always so willing to volunteer their time and do what's right. I know that we raised them right when they offer their help without any suggestions.

"How about you, Josie? I want you to stay in the park

while we're volunteering, but are you going with Daniel or staying by our seats?"

"I'll probably go find some of my friends who are coming to the park to watch the movie with their family. Is that cool, Mom?"

"Sounds good to m—just keep me posted if that changes. I don't want to worry about where you are when we're on popcorn duty."

Jackson

Walking into the kitchen, I give Jules a quick kiss and then head toward the kids. "Hey, guys, good morning. Are you ready to watch the movie in the park tonight?"

"Hey, Daddy, yes, I'm excited! *The Goonies* is one of my favorites. I love watching them figure out the treasure hunt and the piano part."

"Yes, I know. You always loved that, and when they had to walk the plank! I'm looking forward to a nice family night. I like when they do movies in the park. It's always fun to see everyone from town with their families."

I'm just about to pour myself a cup of coffee when my phone buzzes. I look up to see my entire family looking at me with worry. "Dr. Harte," I answered. As I listen to my service tell me that I have a patient heading to the Emergency Room, I let them know that I'm on my way. I look up at my family and try to figure out how to keep this good day on the right track.

"I have to go to the hospital. I'm not sure what I have waiting for me there, but I should be done in time to have our night still. It's only nine o'clock, so don't count me out, okay?"

I look over at Jules, who's hesitant to answer, but then she sees that I'm pleading with her to help smooth over my departure. She looks at the kids, saying, "Dad has plenty of time. Is it a delivery or something not as complicated?"

"Not a delivery, so I should be able to go in, check things out and come back home. I promise to text as soon as I know

156

something."

I walk over and give Jules a quick kiss, then kiss the top of Josie's head and put a hand on Daniel's shoulder. "Daniel, do you have all you need to take Josie and handle our dinner for tonight?"

"Yep, I got it. See you later, Dad."

∞∞∞

Walking into the ER, I learned my call was for one of my pregnant patients who overheated and panicked. She asked the doctor in emergency to have me paged. She just wanted confirmation from her regular doctor that the baby was okay. I look at her chart and agree that the treatment is what I would have recommended myself. I tell her to relax for a day or two, avoid too much lifting, and stay hydrated and out of the heat. She can call and make an appointment for next week if she isn't feeling better. Time to head back home and enjoy the day with my family. I shoot off the text to all of them. Better give them the heads up I'm already done and heading home.

Jackson: Heading home-easy emergency
Jackson: Anyone need me to stop and get anything???
Julia: All good here *heart emoji*
Daniel: NP, got it dad
Josie: See you soon daddy! *heart eyes emojiclapping hands emoji***

When I get home, I find Jules in the yard with Duke. She's walking around, pruning her flowers, and holding some rose cuttings in her hand. "Hi, honey, I'm home."

"Glad it was a quick trip. The kids were so worried it was going to keep you from our evening. I tried to keep them calm, but you know how it's been. They assumed you would miss out."

"I know—thankfully the emergencies have slowed down lately. Do you have time to sit down so I can talk to you?"

"Is everything okay?"

"I have some news, and I think you are going to like it."

"Let me take these flowers and put them in water. Can you grab me a glass of lemonade and meet me on the porch?"

I get us each a glass of lemonade and head out to the porch. I watch while she puts her roses into a pretty vase, washes up, and heads in with a smile.

"I'm here. Spill it, buster. You know I hate secrets."
I look at my gorgeous wife as she sits in front of me with a big smile on her face. "Do you remember Noah? We did our residency in Chicago together. He was going into a more high-end practice in Chicago."

"Noah Roarke? Cute, tall, blonde, lots of muscles?" She says, all breathy and with her lashes fluttering.

"Well, I don't know if I would call him cute, but, yes, that guy." Laughing and shaking my head, I add, "I had a talk with Dad a month ago, and we talked about how I need to make better work and life balance. I needed to figure out a way to do that and do it quickly, so my family wasn't the one suffering from it. While you were seeing Dr. Rose and trying to sort your feelings about what you needed to do to find your happiness, I was actually doing the same."

I watch as Jules wipes a tear away from her face. "Oh, honey, don't cry. You know it takes two to make a problem and to fix it. I needed to work on fixing things on my end and I think I did."

"I know, I still feel so guilty about how I handled things, but I just didn't know what else to do. How to make changes so we could fix our family."

Grabbing Jules's hand and giving it a little squeeze. "While talking to Dad, I realized that with how much the town has expanded, that meant my practice has to grow too. I just couldn't take on the patient load myself anymore. So, I reached out to a couple of doctors that I knew and asked if they would be interested in becoming a partner in my practice."

"Why haven't you mentioned this before, Jackson?

"I wanted to have something to tell you before sharing

that I was working on this. I guess I needed a solution to the problem before I shared the news with you."

"So, is Noah becoming a partner then?"

Smiling, I lean forward, give her a soft kiss, and nod. "Yes, he's ready to get out of the city. He needs a new start and wants to help me with my patient load. He enjoys working with the families, but his practice is so large, he doesn't see a lot of repeat patients. He said not having a stronger connection with his patients is taking away from his love of medicine. He gave his current practice notice; he'll finish this month out, then head this way. He wants time to move to Lake Harmony. He needs to find a house and get a feel for the town. This also gives me time to make an announcement to my patients that we have another doctor starting at the practice and gives us the ability to take on new patients."

"I absolutely LOVE THIS! Noah will be a great addition to your practice and to the town. He is so nice. Is he still married?"

"No, that's also one of the reasons he is ready for a change. His divorce was finalized eight months ago, but they still run in similar circles. He just needs a change since she started dating a mutual friend. He said even though he isn't in love with her anymore, it's just too weird seeing them together at parties and dinners with friends."

"I can only imagine how strange that would be. Very uncomfortable for sure. Once he gets here, we can have dinner and invite the crew over. That way, he can already start making friends our age. My brothers and Cooper will probably get him into poker night. This may be a good solution for both of you."

"I know it will be a great solution for not always being pulled away from my family. We can share the patient load and emergencies that keep me from always missing things. I need to be with you and the kids, especially when you're counting on me."

"Now, how about you tell me where you are, in thinking about your change and if you want to use The Yellow Lady as your business adventure."

Smiling, Jules looks at me. "I have been thinking about it. I decided I'm going to go see Roxie in the Village office and figure out if I can change the zoning on the house to use it for a business. I can't really make too many decisions before I know if it will even be a possibility. If I can do it, I'm not sure if I want to create a Bed and Breakfast business that hosts events or if I make it strictly events and turn the bedrooms into meeting rooms or changing rooms."

"Both great ideas, and I agree that before you get too far into planning, we need to figure out if the house can be used for a business. Are you going to check on the parking situation while you check the zoning?"

"Yes, I have a list of things that I need to get approval for, so when I go into the Village office to see Roxie, I'll make sure that I get any forms that will need to be submitted. I hope they approve it. The house sits far enough away from other homes on that five acres that it won't be a noise or traffic issue. It would be such a beautiful space and location for intimate events."

∞∞∞

We sat on the porch and talked about Noah starting, the kids, and the evening to come. It seems like it has been a while since Jules and I just had the afternoon to ourselves. The kids are back from running out to grab dinner and are working in the kitchen packing our cooler. I hear Daniel tell Josie to grab blankets and bug spray for later. Watching them work together always makes me smile. Even though they're four years apart, they still make a good team. They are awesome kids, and I couldn't be luckier they are mine.

"What car are we driving to town tonight? Mom, should I pack the cooler and chairs up in your SUV or Dad's?"

"Daniel, go ahead and use my car. The chairs are hanging on the hook by the bikes in the garage. Can you manage everything, or do you need Dad to come out?"

"Dad, do you want to help me lift the big cooler in the back of Mom's SUV?"

"Sure thing, let's go."

Once we pack up the car, we all pile in and head to the park where the movie is being shown. Thankfully, we're the first to cover the popcorn station and early to arrive at the park. There is plenty of parking and not too many people are here yet. I expect things will get a bit more crowded in another hour or so after some people eat dinner at home. Josie picks out our spot in the middle of the park, not too close to the speakers. She and Daniel get the chairs and blanket put down. The trick is one blanket under the chairs, so the bugs don't get us after the sun sets. There's a cooler and extra blanket in case anyone gets chilled. With our spot set up and the kids walking off to look for their friends, I grab Jules's hand and head to the popcorn cart. It was borrowed from the 1-Stop General Store, and Gertie is standing there setting it up and waiting for the volunteers to take their shift.

"Jackson and Julia, I believe you are my first volunteers to handle the popcorn. How are you two doing this evening?"

"Gertie, it's nice to see you. Jules and I are great! We're looking forward to the movie and handing out the popcorn. Anything specific we need to know?"

"Popcorn bags are three dollars each or two for five dollars. No change. Trying to keep it simple for you. The cash box is one job and scooping out the popcorn is the second. Who is handling what?"

Jules moves to take the cash box and says she will handle the money and I can handle the popcorn. Gertie explains to me how to take the premixed bag of popcorn and butter and dump it into the popcorn maker. Once it's done popping, we can start scooping popcorn into the paper bags. There really is no measuring, and it looks simple enough. Before Gertie takes off, she makes sure to tell us that we cannot leave the popcorn station until the next team takes our place and we explain how to do the job.

"Have fun, kids. It's nice to see you smiling again, Julia," Gertie walks away with a smirk.

"Oh, jeez, why do I feel like there is going to be something about us on Facebook Harmony Hears tomorrow? Make sure one of us checks in the morning. I'd rather not be surprised."

"I agree, honey. Okay, I'm going to make the first batch. Wish me luck."

∞∞∞

We work our hour shift and enjoy seeing all the families come for the movie in the park night. Many are patients of mine, so the kids get a kick out of Dr. Harte handing out popcorn. Once our shift is over and we pass the popcorn baton to the next shift, it's off to our seats to find the kids so we can have our dinner. The kids have gotten our favorite subs and chips from the deli and brought drinks and chocolate chip cookies for dessert.

"Wow, this looks good. Great choice on the subs. Are they all the same?"

"No, Dad, I got you a roast beef with pepper jack cheese, and Mom has her Italian sub. We figured you always cut them in half and share with each other. We got a variety of chips: BBQ, regular, and salt and vinegar. I wasn't sure if you were going to want popcorn after working at the station. We also have licorice and peanut butter cups for snacking on during the movie."

"You guys did a great job— I'm loving our fifth date!" Jules says to the kids.

"OH NO! Wait!" Josie yells and stands up. "I have to take a picture for evidence. Gram and Auntie Stella told me that's part of the rules. Mom, can I use your phone so you can send it to whoever needs to get the evidence?"

Laughing, I hand her my phone and watch her take probably twenty pictures. Of course, before she can give my phone back to

162

me, Gertie walks by. "Look at the Harte Family. Looking cute in your matching t-shirts. Do you want me to take a family picture of all of you?"

Josie hands my phone over to her with a huge smile and says, "Thank you, Miss Gertie, that would be so great!"

Gertie takes our family picture, then asks if she can have a copy for Facebook to post on Harmony Hears. *Sure, why not.* I tell her to go ahead and text herself the picture.

We enjoy our dinner, and, as we're eating, many of our friends walk by and say hello to us. Some of the kids' friends stop and ask if they want to join them but they both politely say no because it's our family date night. Not even Jules's parents, siblings, or friends join us. They are near but giving us our time as a family. As the sun goes down, there's an announcement that the movie will begin in fifteen minutes. We watch everyone do a last-minute mad dash to get more popcorn and quick trips to the parked cars for things forgotten, and then we settle in and prepare to watch the movie. To the right of us, I see Ruby and Edison, smiling and looking at their phones. Ruby looks over at us and points to her phone. Then I see Jules reach for her phone and laugh.

"Jackson, look at this. Gertie doesn't waste any time." She hands over her phone, and I see the Harmony Hears Facebook post with our family picture.

Family Movie Night In The Park

If you're not in Harmony Park tonight for the showing of The Goonies you are missing out! There is still time to get here before the movie starts promptly at dusk. The Hartes of Harmony are here, dressed in movie star style with their matching shirts!

I look at Gertie's Facebook post, and I love the idea of a play on words with 'Harte of Harmony,' and an idea starts brewing in my head. "Jules, what do you think of Harte of Harmony for your business name? Since you're making it an intimate venue, that could be a great choice. Playing off your name and it also showcases the type of venue you want it to reference."

"Oh, that is a fun idea. Let's not forget that. I love it!"

Chapter Twenty-Nine

Julia

What a great time we all had this weekend spending time as a family and watching *Goonies* movie in the park. I stretch my arms over my head and think about what the week will bring. My to-do list involves heading to the Village Hall offices and talking to Roxie about what we need to do to turn the Yellow Lady from a home into a business. She'll be able to guide me through all the steps I have to take since she is the Village Manager. I can't get too excited until I figure out whether the beautiful home can be switched from a residential to a business zone. *Well, let's get this party started and get ready for Monday, Jules. Time's a wastin'.*

I quickly get up and jump in the shower and prepare for the day. The kids have plans with their friends today so I can focus on what I need to do. First stop, coffee with Ellen at Harmonious Bites to enjoy coffee with my sister until the Village opens for business. I take the time to deep condition my hair and use a new lavender vanilla sugar scrub that Stella made. She really needs to start selling her products. I dry off, get dressed quickly, and dry my hair. I never did wear a lot of make-up, but I add some mascara and blush to my cheekbones. The weather is nice, so I put on my sundress and head down to the kitchen. The house is quiet, so the kids must still be in bed.

Duke is sleeping at the top of the stairs, "Come on, buddy, let's get you outside and give you some food." He jumps up and wobbles down the stairs in front of me. That silly dog is waiting at the back door, and it's like he is smiling at me, saying *Come on, Mom, I need to go out and investigate the yard.* I open the door, and out he runs, doing his perimeter check before taking care of business. I walk to the pantry and fill his bowl with kibble and give him some fresh water. Crazy dog. I love him so much. He was one of the pups from Mom and Dad's neighbor. They thought I was crazy for taking a Great Pyrenees for a house dog. All their dogs are working dogs. Duke is a working dog. He keeps us safe from birds, leaves, delivery men, and the occasional squirrel. I've never had such an amazing dog. Outside breed or not, he is my shadow, and I would be a fool not to love on him as much as possible. The kids like to tease me that I love the dog more than them. *Sometimes!* I think to myself. He loves me no matter what and doesn't talk back, I tease them.

Once the dog is back inside, I grab my purse and head to Harmonious Bites for a quick breakfast and to chat with my sister.

∞∞∞

I walk into the shop and see Ellen behind the counter, "Good morning! How are you doing today?"

"Hey, sis, you look pretty this morning. Where are you off to all dressed up so early?"

"I came to have coffee with you until I can head over to the Village office and talk to Roxie about something. Do you have time to join me while I have my coffee?"

"Yep, just give me a sec to make your usual and grab us a scone. Go grab our table, and I'll bring it over and join you."

I see our usual table in the back is free, so I head over and take a seat. I brought my notes with me about what I am thinking of doing, so I want to talk to Ellen about my ideas while we enjoy our coffee. She grew up in the same house I did with a dad who owns his own construction business, so she may have some ideas that I haven't thought of yet. I look up and see her walking over with a tray and a big smile.

"Here we go. I wasn't sure which scone you'd want, so I grabbed two different ones. Halfsies? I brought lemon and cranberry orange."

"Yummy!"

"So, you're heading over to the village. What do you need to do there with Roxie?"

I sit there biting my lip, a bit nervous. So far, no one knows that we own the Yellow Lady except the former owners. Here goes! "Jackson and I own the Yellow Lady." I sat back and let her absorb that news.

"Wow! I didn't know that was even in the works. How did this all come about?"

"Growing up, Jackson and I always loved that house. We would dream about one day owning it, raising a family there, and enjoying that beautiful house up on the bluff. She always felt so majestic and magical. When he found out it was going on the market, he bought it for me. Honestly, Ellen, I had no idea. It was just one of those things when you do something crazy. But you know what? I kind of love it. We talked about it a lot over the weekend, and we both feel fate dropped her into our laps."

"Are you going to live there? I know how much you adore your home and neighborhood."

"No, I think I have a better use for her, and that is what I need to talk to Roxie about today."

"Jules, come on…you can't leave it like that. Spill right now before I lose it. What exactly are you going to do with her?"

"I am going to open my own business, and I need to find out if I can use the Yellow Lady as my home base for the business before I make any bigger plans."

"That is so exciting! I'm so happy for you. Wow, I feel like you're on fire these days, and that makes me happy. I am so glad that Dr. Rose seems to have really helped you, Julia. I was so worried about you, and Jackson too. I know how much you love each other and seeing you so sad broke my heart. I know she really helped us when Scott and I realized that starting a family the traditional way was not going to be our path. But enough about that—tell me everything!"

"I brought my notes and was hoping you could brainstorm with me and tell me if I missed anything. After talking with Mom and Jackson, I think I've narrowed it down to two different ideas. I love the idea of keeping it a home and maybe turning it into a Bed and Breakfast. It is such a beautiful home and location, so I want as many people to enjoy it as possible. The other idea is to make it into a more intimate venue. Small weddings and smaller events that could use the house and the grounds."

I look up at my sister as I wait for a response from her. I'm biting my lip, trying not to say anything while I wait for her to think about what she wants to say. One thing I have learned (and love) about my sister, Ellen, is that she always thinks about what she is going to say before she says it. I watch her and can almost see the wheels turning. I'm about to say something when she smiles and looks at me.

"Jules, why can't you do both? You may not always have an event, but you could always use it as a B & B. Let's say you have a small wedding that is scheduled with you. Friday night is usually the rehearsal, Saturday the wedding, and then Sunday morning a lot of people like to have an intimate breakfast with their immediate family before everyone heads home. So, you have the wedding on the grounds, and you have the Bed and Breakfast for some of the family to stay together on site."

"Hmm, I never thought of that. I guess it would depend on the type of event and if they need the entire space."

"You can make it to where the downstairs has multiple uses—meetings or small gatherings. You already have the kitchen, so you could provide simple meals or hire Hillary to cater the bigger stuff. Not all rooms have to be bedrooms either. You can make one a dressing room or conference room for smaller meetings. There are a lot of multi-uses you could do. If you have a larger wedding, you can always use a big tent structure on the land in the gardens."

"Ellen, you are exactly what I needed this morning! I had so many ideas but couldn't seem to put them together to give me the whole picture. I think you are on to something. Can I come to you again and brainstorm once I have the big things in place?"

"Honey, you can always come to me. That's what family is for, and you don't even need to ask."

I lean over and give her a big hug. "Love you."

"Love you too, Jules."

We finish our coffee, and I head over to see Roxie at the Village offices. I have my plan in place, and now I just need to make sure I can do everything I hope I can with the Yellow Lady.

Walking into the Village office, I head straight to the Village Manager's office to find Roxie. "Good morning, Roxie. Hope you had a good weekend."

"Well, looky here—good morning, Julia. It's a nice surprise to see you here. What can I do for you?"

"Roxie, I need to know what I have to do to make a residential home into a business. Is this something that you can help me with? I know I need to look at zoning and permits, but I want to be able to leave here with all the paperwork so I can get it submitted as soon as possible."

"Yes, dear, you're in the right place. First, I need to know what location we're talking about. That's the first step. Do you have a place in mind? Is this for your dad and Stone Builders?"

With butterflies in my stomach, I think about how I'm going to answer. Roxie is one of the Widows Crew and hangs out with Gertie. Whatever I'm about to share will go directly to Gertie's ears, so I need to be cautious. I don't want details going out before I'm ready.

"The property is The Yellow Lady. Jackson and I bought it from Mr. and Mrs. Phillips. They're downsizing, and they wanted to keep the Yellow Lady in good hands. Jackson made them an offer and, well, next thing you know, we own her!"

Smiling at me, Roxie says, "I see! I knew she was sold but I wasn't sure who had bought her. We know how everyone feels about that home. It's like the queen of Lake Harmony up on the bluff watching over us."

"Yes, Jackson and I have always dreamed of owning her. I just need to see if it's possible to change the zoning and what steps we need to take for it to be a business site."

"Easy enough, and it should be fine since she sits on about five acres. She has her own access road, so that will help with zoning too. Let me get all the forms you'll need so you can get started on them. When you're done, bring them back in to be submitted for approval with the village because this will need to go through an approval process before you can do more. Do you know what you want to do with her yet? What kind of business are you doing? Oh, is Jackson moving out of the town square?"

"No, not Jackson. This is something that I may do myself. Still working out the details, and I don't want to share too much until I have a better idea of everything."

"Okay, Julia, let me put all the zoning and permit paperwork in a file folder for you. If you have any questions about filling them out, please feel free to reach out to me. I believe they are simple enough to understand."

"Thank you so much, Roxie. I will get these back to you this week. I want to make sure we have all the approvals we need before making too many more decisions."

On my way out of the Village offices, I decide to walk across the park and to Jackson's office. Maybe I can steal him between patients. I stop at the 1-Stop General store on my way over and grab us some sandwiches and potato salad for an early lunch.

"Hi, Peter. Hi, Gertie—how are the both of you doing today?"

"Julia, it's so nice to see you. Thank you for working the popcorn cart this weekend for the movie night. We managed to raise over six hundred dollars to go towards the fountain and garden repairs."

"Peter, that is great news! Hopefully, the pranksters have learned their lesson. I wanted to stop in and grab a couple of sandwiches and some of Gertie's potato salad to take over to

Jackson for lunch."

I watch Peter go back behind the deli area and wash his hands. "What can I get you then. Same as usual? Roast beef and pepper jack for Jackson and Italian for you?"

"Yes, for Jackson, but can you make mine a tuna salad on rye? I know Gertie always makes a batch on Mondays."

"Let me get those started for you."

While Peter is making the sandwiches, I grab two drinks for us and watch as Gertie gives me a bigger container of potato salad than what I need. She walks over with a smile on her face.

"So, Julia, thank you for letting me use that family picture from the movie. What a lovely family you have, dear. I love seeing you with a smile on your face again."

I smile back and pause before speaking, "It was a lovely night, and I was very happy we were able to enjoy a family night together. Jackson has been pretty busy with work lately, but we're working on making some changes that will give him some more family time."

"Oh… anything you want to share?" Gertie says with a sparkle of mischief.

Laughing, I reply, "Oh, Gertie, no scoop for you yet for Harmony Hears, but soon."

"Gertie, leave Julia alone. She isn't in here for you to grab your gossip."

"Peter, I'm just making sure our lovely Julia is okay. I'm allowed to do that. I have known her most of her life."

"I love that you both worry about me, but I can honestly tell you I'm doing great. So please, don't worry. All good things, good changes are coming. I will give you one scoop, though, Gertie. I know who the new owners of the Yellow Lady are."

I try to keep my face neutral and not give anything away immediately, but the way Gertie's eyes light up and I can see her gossip wheels waiting to spring, I bite my lip to keep from laughing.

"Dear, if you don't spill the news immediately, I will take that potato salad back."

"Gertie, the new owners are locals."

"JULIA!"

Now laughing, I lean forward and say, "Me. I own the Yellow Lady."

"What? What do you mean, you own the Yellow Lady?" Gertie isn't putting it together, so I better just give her a little more even though I know it will be on Facebook before I even reach Jackson's office. "Jackson bought her for me. We have always loved that house. We grew up hoping one day we would have our family in that home. He spoke with Mr. Philips, and since they had hoped the home would go to someone that loves her, they made a deal, and Jackson and I own her now."

Gertie has the biggest smile on her face. One I haven't seen for a bit. Peter comes back to the counter with my sandwiches in hand. "That is wonderful news. You know we are always worried about out-of-towners coming in and making a mess of our little town and lake. Are you going to move out to the house then?"

"No, I have bigger and better plans for her, but that is all I can share with you at this point."

I grab our lunch, say goodbye to Gertie and Peter, and make my way across the square to Jackson's office. As I walk in, I greet the front desk, and they buzz me back to Jackson's office. Paige walks out of a room, and I say hello. She tells me Jackson is just finishing up with a patient, and she will let him know I am in his office with lunch.

Waiting in my husband's office, I walk around and notice that he has pictures of us all over his office. He's even added a few new ones, including the picture he printed of us from our movie in the park. He must have printed that off the Facebook post. He is surrounded by us, and even has a picture of Duke. Smiling, I keep looking around and hear the door open behind me.

"This is a great surprise, honey. Are you going to tell me why you have that big smile on your face?"

I turn around and put my arms around my husband and look up into his eyes. "I love you. That is why I have this big smile on my face."

"I love you, too, and I'm happy to put that smile on your face. Did I do something to earn it?"

"Yes, I was just looking around your office and noticed you have pictures of all of us surrounding you."

"Honey, I have to have you all around me. There are days I am sitting here, buried in paperwork, and working late. I guess I felt that if I couldn't be home with all of you, I at least needed to have you here with me. Even Duke!"

"Yes, I saw that! I brought us some lunch. Do you have time to eat quickly or do you want me to put it in the fridge for a little later?"

"Perfect timing. I just finished up my morning patients, and the front office is demanding that I take an hour for lunch each day since Paige told them it is no longer allowed to add patients into my lunch or after four o'clock. So, that means I can eat with you and enjoy an hour with my beautiful wife."

I get our sandwiches out and give us each some potato salad. As we're eating, I tell Jackson I started the day with Ellen and the talk we had about the business idea and the Yellow Lady.

"Ellen and I talked about creating a venue that is a Bed and Breakfast *and* has the ability to be an intimate event venue. She had some great ideas, and I think I'm going to build off those. After I leave here, I'm going home to make a rough business plan. I went to see Roxie and I told her and Gertie that we own the Yellow Lady but want to make it a business, not a residential home. She gave me zoning and permit paperwork to fill out. So, once we have that piece done and approved, we can start talking about what we will actually do with the Yellow Lady."

"Looks like it is all slowly coming together. My question to you is, how do YOU feel about it? Is this the dream you see for yourself?"

I take a minute and think about what Jackson asked me. *Do I think having a small event business will satisfy my need for having a purpose? Will it make me happy? I think so!* Smiling, I look at my husband, concern on his face as he awaits my reply. "Honey, I actually think that I could make this into something wonderful. I have a decent starting point, but I do need to sit down and think about all the details. I can reach out to Dad and Rob and ask them about any building and remodeling, Hillary will have great knowledge about the catering aspect of it all, and with your support and brainstorming, I feel like I can do anything."

"I'm thrilled that this is making you feel happy again and giving you something exciting to focus on. I just want to make sure this is what you really want and not that you are just trying to fill a hole."

"No, I'm truly excited about the idea of having my own event venue and making special moments for people. You know how much I love to take a moment and make it unforgettable."

After we finish lunch, Jackson tells me he wants to help me fill out the forms for the zoning and permits when he gets home. Once we have them submitted for approval, we can finally move forward and take the next steps. As I'm cleaning up the garbage from our lunch, I get a text from Stella.

Stella: OMG JULES!!!!
Stella: I am so excited for you
Stella: Can't wait to hear deets
Julia: What are you talking about???
Stella: YL
Julia: ???
Stella: *annoyed emoji* YELLOW LADY OWNER
Julia: Oh yes! So exciting
Julia: Heading home now if you want deets come by
Stella: YES! C U soon

I stand up and grab my purse and the folder from the Village with all my forms. "Honey, I'm heading home now. That was Stella—she is SO excited and heading to our house now to talk about the Yellow Lady. I'll see you after work."

"Thank you for lunch, Jules. I love you."

He pulls me in for a hug and a soft kiss on my lips. "I love you too, honey."

$$\infty \infty \infty$$

As I arrive home from lunch with Jackson and pull into the garage, I already see Stella in her pink jeep pull in behind me. I get out of the car and watch her glide up the drive to me.

"Hey, sis, I'm so excited to hear the plan!"

"Stella, how exactly are you so in the know about the Yellow Lady anyway?"

"Silly, Gertie posted about it on Harmony Hears."

I groan to myself. Boy, that woman didn't even take a day to post the gossip. She is on fire. "Let's go in so I can see what fuss she made about it."

Stella loops her arm through mine, and we go inside. Duke is always happy for company, so he is bouncing around Stella as she walks to the dog treats.

"Hi, Dukey, can you sit like a good boy for Auntie Stella to give you kisses and a treat?"

That dog drops down so fast, I have to laugh. He is a very food-motivated dog.

"Want a lemonade?" I ask her.

"Sure, sounds great."

I watch as she walks to the porch with Duke and sits on the porch swing. I put the forms on the counter from the Village, so they don't get in the way until later and grab us both a lemonade to drink while we chat on the porch.

"So, you said Gertie posted something? Can you pull it up for me, please? I left my phone in my purse."

Stella grabs her phone and hands it to me to read.

BREAKING NEWS…Yellow Lady New Owners Revealed
The Yellow Lady, the beautiful Victorian home, which sits majestically on the bluff overlooking Lake Harmony, has been purchased by new owners. Lucky for us, they are current

residents and very respected. **The buzz is that the home will not be used as a family residence but rather a business. No word yet on what type of business, but knowing who is taking the lead on it, I have no doubt it will enhance the town, not stress it out. Good luck to the new owners - our "hartes" are with you.**

Oh, that woman! I look at Stella. "Really? Our hartes are with you? She couldn't just say Jackson and Julia own the house?"

"You know she gets a kick out of being clever. So...what do you have to share? You know I can't wait for secrets to be shared. I guess that happens when you're the youngest. No one ever tells me anything."

I tell Stella whatever I know at this point. It feels good sharing the news and talking about what we're planning with the house. It won't be easy, but I think we can pull this together.

"Jules, who is going to run the Bed and Breakfast? I mean, I know it is your business, but you need someone on-site at all times, right?"

Oh, I hadn't thought about that part yet. I get up and grab my paperwork, where I have some ideas and notes written down about the house portion of the business idea.

"You're right. I can't be there 24/7, so I will need to figure out how to hire an onsite coordinator or Innkeeper person. I better add that to the list of things to think about."

"Well, if you're in a pinch, I'm happy to help out wherever I can, but don't worry about it yet. One thing at a time."

Stella and I continue to talk about my business plan I'm working on and what is going on with the kids. She fills me in on having enough of her bath salts and that she's now added oils and soaps that she is selling at a weekend farmer's market booth.

"Speaking of your products, Stella. I think you have a great thing going with these things. The last time I took a bath with the lavender salts you made me, I could have fallen asleep in the tub. I was so relaxed and really enjoyed it. Jackson even said how great the upstairs smelled from it. We both slept like a rock that night."

She looks happy and maybe a bit surprised at what I said. "I am so glad you're enjoying it, Jules. I'm having a lot of fun making things. I sell out almost every weekend at the market. Sometimes, I even have requests for items if I'm sold out."

"Do you think you'd be interested in keeping the guest rooms filled with your soap and lotions? We could even set up a small space in the main house where you could sell them."

My little sister starts to bounce in her seat. "Are you SERIOUS!? YES, yes, yes!"

Her products have been amazing, so why wouldn't I want to support her. "Of course, Stella. I love you, and the products are awesome. I'm proud of you."

Chapter Thirty

Julia

I'm heading to Dr. Rose's office for my last session. We only scheduled this far out when I initially went to see her. I know that if I need to schedule more, I can, but I'm in a better place than I was when I first went to see her. With a little bounce in my step, I walk into her office and wait for her to open the door. I'm looking through all the earlier journal pages that I have been using and can read how far I have come. I love how much the date assignment she suggested has helped Jackson and I reconnect. We've been able to communicate better and see that he was even able to make some personal changes himself so that he isn't so stressed out all the time. I read over the entry I made last night.

Monday-7 weeks

Life:
Jackson and I are stronger than we were a month ago. We have reconnected not only with our time together but also intimately. If he is in the room, he is either touching me or his eyes are never far from watching me. He makes love to me often. Sometimes with such a desire, it's like he will die if he can't have me. Other times, it's gentle and loving as if I will break. We send simple but loving texts to each other throughout the day. Always making a determined point in keeping this new connection strong and fueled. I love him more than the first time I told him I loved him, the first time we made love, the moment I said I do. He is my other half, and as he so often tells me, I am his. The kids are happy, too. Life has gone back to happy days and

steamy nights for us.

Business:
*She is slowly coming together. Jackson and I own the Yellow Lady!
I still can't believe my crazy husband bought that house for me
without discussing it, but he did it out of love and fulfilling a dream.
We dreamed of owning her, having her as we grow old. She may not
become our family home, but she is going to hopefully become my
business. I want to shine her up and make her the majestic beauty
she is and share her with as many others as possible. She has a
romantic glow that surrounds her, and I hope to bring that part of
the house back to life. She is simply magnificent and must be shared
with anyone wishing to step inside and enjoy her.*

"Julia, are you ready?" Dr. Rose says with a smile from her
office.

"Whoops, lost in my journal." I stand and enter the office
and take a seat. Dr. Rose shuts the door behind us and sits across
from me.

"I must say, Julia, I think you're radiating happiness right
now. Care to share what has that smile on your face?"

I talked to Dr. Rose about the journal entry I was just
rereading from yesterday. She asks me about how things are
going between Jackson and I and him and the kids. I told her
about the Movie in the Park date that became a family outing.

"We broke the rules a little bit, but the kids wanted in on
the date planning."

"Well, I wouldn't say you "broke rules" because there
weren't any. The point of the assignment was to spend time
together, communicate, and reconnect. The fact that your
family and friends took it a step further only shows how much
love surrounds the both of you. Honestly, I love that they all
took over planning the dates. That allowed you to focus on being
together and not about proving a point. It seems to have worked
beautifully."

"Yes, it was a lot of fun, and I realize there are a lot of

people in my life that want the best for us and love us both very much. They all showed us that we're not alone in this life. That we can and should reach out for support when we need it. I'm beyond blessed to have so many amazing people in my life."

"Yes, I'm very glad you are where you are and that things are so positive. Now, we talked about the family side of things. That wasn't where you still felt a hole. Have you gotten anywhere with what will fill it? I know the last time we talked; you were thinking about starting a business. Do you want to talk about how that is going?"

I share all the information I can about how Jackson bought the Yellow Lady and how we submitted all our paperwork to the Village Hall to see if we could change the home into a business.

When my session is about over, Dr. Rose smiles and looks up at me. "Julia, I think you're on to great things. It sounds like you have a good balance with family, and now you have an exciting plan for a business. Do you feel like you have a purpose now? Like this is something that you are meant to do?"

"Yes, I'm really excited about all the possibilities with this idea. Not everything is planned out completely, but I have a plan, and now I have something that brings me joy. I realize that I'm the only one keeping myself from feeling lost. I learned that I need to make some time for myself and not feel guilty about it. I feel happy again. Excited for what is in front of me."

We finished the session, and Dr. Rose said if I ever need her to just pick up the phone and schedule a session. I should keep journaling because that is a great way to write down what I'm feeling and easy enough to refer to it for reflection. I thank her for all her help and head home.

∞∞∞

That evening after dinner, Jackson and I sat on the porch with our drinks. We talk about waiting for the paperwork to clear.

Luckily with our small town and everyone putting pressure on the Village because they can't wait to see what becomes of the Yellow Lady, we shouldn't have to wait too long for approvals. Roxie said that she did some homework herself after I left her office Monday, and, after speaking to the different zoning and permit divisions, she didn't think we would have any issues with making it a business location. Since it has five acres and its own access road, there aren't other homes or businesses that it would interfere with. So, we're optimistic that things will push through without issue.

"Honey, how are you feeling about everything right now? I know you had your last appointment with Dr. Rose today. Do you want to talk about it?"

I lean my head against his shoulder. "I'm happy and excited. To be honest, though, I am a little nervous about all the details. I haven't done this before, creating a business. I feel a little bit overwhelmed. I am not one hundred percent sure I know how to get my ducks in a row on this. You know?"

"I know you have a general idea of what you want to do. Do you want to brainstorm? Get it more detailed and the little things figured out. Would that help put your mind at ease?"

"That would be great. I think if I have a better business plan in place, that will help me work through the details."

"Then that is exactly what we need to do." Jackson gives me a kiss and says, "Trust me?"

"Always."

I watch him get up and walk into the kitchen. He grabs his phone and mine and comes back onto the porch. He hands me my phone and then starts typing away on his phone. My phone buzzes in my hand, so I look down and read it.

Jackson: Date 6-Planning Session-TYL (Friends & Family)
Jackson: I need all those reading this to attend a mandatory meeting
Rob: FIVE dates dude- 5, not 6
Garrett: Shut it Rob-please go on J
Jackson: Julia and I have an announcement and need your help
Julia: Nothing bad *smiley emoji* we promise

Hillary: Jeezus! Jackson way to scare us all *eye roll emoji*
Dad Harte: Mom and I are there son-when?
Jackson: Sunday, 6pm, our house-BBQ and planning
Jackson: Chicken and Steak Provided
Hillary: I will bring some sides (Salad, corn, watermelon?)
Ellen: Yay, I've got taco dip - Scott said beer
Rob: Chips
Garrett: Big splurge brother *laughing emoji*
Mom Stone: Dad and I will bring some wine and lemon bars
Rob: Bite me
Dad Stone: Rob- watch it
Rob: Sorry everyone *Sad emoji*
Cooper: I've got jalapeño poppers
Bree: Dessert
Stella: *heart emoji**heart emoji**heart emoji*
Sam: Paul and I will bring more beer
Griffin: Jacks you always have the meat *wink emoji*
Jackson: *laughing emoji* Thank you everyone-no worries tho

"Honey, we're all set. Everyone that loves you is going to be here Sunday for dinner and to help us brainstorm. I figured your dad and brothers would be helpful in discussing any remodeling that will need to be done. Sam and Paul will be helpful in getting the gardens in shape. Hillary and Griffin will be good to talk about any catering needs. Bree is just so damn organized—she can help you keep it all together. Our parents because are older and wiser than the two of us. Coop because he knows EVERYONE in this town too. I think that covers it."

"What, no Gertie? The town gossip isn't included in that list of people?" Laughing, I lean over and kiss him. "I love you, my crazy husband, and thank you for loving me so much that you just invited our entire family and crazy crew over."

"I would do anything for you, and if this will keep you moving forward and excited, then that is what we will do."

"Thank you."

"I have one more thing to share with you. I think we have a starting date for Noah. He is going to begin looking for a house next week. I'm hoping that he will be ready to go in a month or so. His current practice asked him to stay on a little longer because they don't have the bandwidth in the schedule to move his current patients over to someone new, so he agreed. He wants to find a house now, though, so he can close and be here when he starts. He figured if he has to commute for a few weeks, it won't be an issue, but he wants to move as soon as possible."

Chapter Thirty-One

Julia

It's Sunday morning, and our entire family and group of friends are coming over to help us plan the next steps with the business, using the Yellow Lady as an intimate venue for smaller events. All anyone has gotten out of us so far is that we own the house, and I plan on using it for a business. Ellen and Stella have been pretty good at not sharing what kind of business. The more I've thought about this, creating a smaller and more intimate location for events and parties, the more excited I'm getting. Jackson and I were lucky enough to get a verbal go-ahead from the village office. We just need to wait for the next village board meeting for it to push through officially, but it all looks good to go.

Dad was also a huge help because he knows all the village board members along with most of the building inspectors because of Stone's Builders and the fact that he's built most of the new homes in town. I secretly think Dad put a little push in the approval process for me, but I'm not complaining. The town is excited and hopes that creating another venue space here will also bring more money into the local businesses.

Jackson and Daniel went to the gym together this morning. I love that he's starting to make new ways to connect with our son. It doesn't hurt that Daniel gets a kick out of trying to outdo Jackson with weights and running distance. The last time they came home, my husband looked like he was ready to drop. I still chuckle thinking about him trying to outperform our son, who is sixteen and used to football practice and hard-core strength training. At least they're enjoying some guy time together. Josie's been having ice cream runs with him at the Freeze Hut, too. They don't think we know, but it's hard to miss when they both come home and look guilty for not bringing us treats, ice cream drips on their shirts.

Sitting on the porch, writing in my journal, I'm making notes about how I feel, and now I can add things that pop into my thoughts about what I want to do with the Yellow Lady. Jackson and I already both agree that we're going to rename her Harte of Harmony. Of course, to most residents, she'll always be the Yellow Lady. That'll never change, and her color will also remain the same. She's a local icon and to change her appearance drastically would ruin her. She'll get a coat of new paint and a freshened-up yard, but for the most part, she will remain the majestic lady on the bluff.

I have time before everyone shows up, and we got the keys in hand yesterday, so Jackson and I are going to do our first walk-through today. We wanted to give Mr. and Mrs. Phillips time to pack their belongings and move without interruption because we know how much they loved that house and the many memories we know they are leaving behind. Going prior to them moving their things out just felt like an intrusion, so Jackson and I have purposely left them alone. Before the closing on the house, we did have an inspection done just to see what types of things would need attention. Thankfully, they maintained that home like an extension of the family, and she is in pristine condition. They already had the electric and plumbing updated as needed. The house is in great shape for being such an old home.

I hear Jackson come in from the garage with Daniel, and it makes me so happy to listen to them talking like buddies and joking around. Jackson comes around the corner looking for me. "Hi, did you have a good morning?"

"Hi, honey, yep, just sitting here writing some thoughts down. Are you still up for heading over and looking at her?"

"Absolutely! I cleaned up at the gym before we left so that

I'm ready to go and all yours today."

"Let's just let the kids know we are heading out for a little bit."

I head up to Josie's room and tell her we're leaving and to make sure to clean up any mess she makes while we're out. The kids both know that we are going to have a house full of people for dinner. I find Daniel in his room and peek my head in, "Hey, buddy, Dad and I are heading out to look at the house really quick. Can you stick around for a while for Josie until we get back?"

"Sure, Mom, no problem. I'll be home. Have fun."

Heading back down to grab my purse, I stop and take a moment on the stairs. I'm so excited to finally go see her, and while I'm distracted and lost in my thoughts standing halfway down the stairs, Jackson comes and stands at the bottom, smiling at me.

"Hey, sorry, I'm coming. I just let the kids know we were leaving. I didn't mean to keep you waiting."

"No rush, I just heard you coming down and then stop, so I wanted to make sure you were okay. Then when I saw you and that smile stretched across your face, I knew you were fine. I have to say, sweetheart, I love seeing that smile and the sparkle back in your eyes. Are you ready to go see your future business?"

"I'm SO ready! Let's go check her out."

Driving over in the car, Jackson is holding my hand and his thumb is moving back and forth over it. I love how touchy-feely he is with me. Always making sure that I am aware of him lately. *I see you making the effort and I love it.*

We make our way up the long drive, and as we drive through the trees, the Yellow Lady comes into view. I gasp, realizing that she is now ours. We dreamed of being able to drive up to her and walk right in the front door for so many years. To have this be our reality right now has me giggle out loud.

Jackson parks the car in the drive, and we both sit looking at her until he turns, "Care to share your thoughts, Jules?"

"I can't believe she's ours. Pulling up to her just now and

then thinking about how you bought her without even telling me, and now...to have her for myself to create a business. I...just...I can't really believe it. Is this my life?"

"Yeah, baby, this is all for you. Are you happy?"

"I'm so happy right now; I'm about to explode. Let's go, Jackson! I can't wait another minute!"

We walk hand in hand up to the front door, but before going in, I turn and stand there on the porch looking down at Lake Harmony. Watching the boats moving across the water, it feels like coming home. I am so overwhelmed standing here on the front porch, my hand over my mouth, with tears in my eyes.

Jackson moves up behind me and puts his arms around me and his chin down onto my shoulder. "I would do anything for you, Jules. You are the love of my life, and without you and the kids, nothing else matters. We dreamed of this moment and this house all those years ago. It may not have happened as we thought, but we have her now, and I know you're going to make this a place where other people's dreams come true."

"Thank you, honey. Thank you for believing in me, in us." I turn in his arms and put my hands on his face. "I love you so much," I say and then kiss my husband. "Let's go inside."

He hands me the key. "I'm going to let you do the honors of opening the door."

I open the door and walk into the Yellow Lady and turn in a full circle, taking in the front foyer, beautiful wood floors, crown molding, and the grand staircase. Moving slowly through the big empty rooms, holding Jackson's hand, we take it all in. We move through from room to room, and I can already see the changes materialize in my thoughts. If we could open the formal dining room and large library into one large space, we could hold small weddings inside or small gatherings with tables. The front parlor with its beautiful ornate fireplace would be a great spot for brides to have their pictures taken or a small intimate dinner for a special occasion. The second parlor in the back of the house, closer to the kitchen, would serve as the perfect office for me.

The Philips's had added a master suite to the first floor,

and that would be perfect if we did hire a manager for the business to live on site. The kitchen would need some updating and new appliances. There's a beautiful little sun porch off the kitchen area that has a lovely view to the lake with a cute octagonal sitting area attached. This would be a charming spot to set up breakfast for any guests.

I turn around and give him a big smile. "I have so many ideas running through my head right now. This is so lovely. I can't even believe it. Let's go upstairs and look at the bedrooms."

As we walk up the stairs, I slide my hand along the beautiful wood railing of the grand staircase. I imagine brides and their wedding party lining up here, or large families lined up, from oldest to youngest, for a family portrait. The upstairs landing is similar in size and overlooks the foyer. *We need a beautiful chandelier to hang here. Something that will cast sparkles into the foyer.*

There are five bedrooms on this floor and a bright, open room that is the same size and shape in the turret that the garden room has downstairs. This would be a beautiful space for a bride preparing for her groom. *Bridal suite...hmm?* We walk through the bedrooms one by one. They all have wood floors that have signs of many years of use but can be easily shined and polished. Each bedroom has a small bath attached—small and simple but clean and updated. That will be an excellent addition to make these guest quarters. Moving to the back of the house, I see another smaller staircase leading up and down.

"Honey, I never realized that there's a third floor in this house, did you?"

"No, I figured it was just an attic space but let's go have a look and see how you can use it later."

We both make our way up and are happily surprised that this floor must have been used for the kids. There isn't a bathroom on this level, but it is a large room with natural light coming in through the windows. I'm not sure how I will use this room, but it is a lot of extra space with a ton of possibilities.

We make our way back down and sit at the bottom of the

grand staircase.

Jackson takes my hand. "Jules, what do you think? I can see the wheels turning, and I am dying a little here."

We're sitting close enough that I can lay my head on his shoulder. "I think this is going to be absolutely perfect. The room off the kitchen in the turret could be made so cute with little bistro tables for guests to sit. There is enough room in the garden porch to add more tables and even some comfortable couches. Keep it light and airy and just peaceful. The kitchen needs an update, especially if we're cooking for guests staying here. The rest seems to be just cosmetic. Some paint and small touch-ups would bring her back to sparkling quickly."

"I agree. Mr. and Mrs. Phillips kept her in great shape for all these years."

"Jackson, I think she will be perfect for what I want to do." Looking up at my husband. "I'm still nervous. Do you really think I can do this? Should I take this risk?"
Putting his arm around me and kissing my temple, he pulls away and says, "First of all, YOU aren't doing anything alone. You have me and everyone who loves you there to support you whenever you need it. I have no doubt whatsoever that you can make this a success. Look at everything that you've already done, Jules. The events and parties that you have organized or hosted. You can do this, and I will be at your side, supporting you at every turn."

"Okay, then let's do this! Let's look at the gardens and see what needs to be freshened up outside."

We hold hands and walk around the house. I can tell that the focus was on keeping the inside of the house in pristine shape, but the gardens and yard were too much upkeep for the older owners. The beds all need to be cleaned up, bushes pruned, and flowers planted. The fountain that sits in the rose garden needs to be fixed, and a fresh pump put in, but overall, it seems to be mostly just normal fixing and nothing that would be a money pit. The stairs that lead down to the private beach will also need to be evaluated and most likely replaced. Otherwise, we don't have too much once we open the middle rooms into one space.

"Okay, I think I have a good starting point so we can talk with everyone, share the ideas I have, and get some feedback on how to handle getting her ready to go!"

∞∞∞

Once we get home, I start getting the house ready for all our family and friends to arrive. Daniel and Jackson have run out to get ice for the coolers, and they got the chicken and steak seasoned and marinating. Since I am a nervous wreck, I grab a glass of water and head to the yard. I have about an hour or so before everyone arrives. "Come on, Duke! Let's go outside." The dog jumps up so quickly, he runs me over heading to the back door. "Okay, buddy, let's get some of that energy out before we have a house full of people."

I'm barely in the yard when I hear Stella.

"Jules, I'm here early. What do you need me to do?"

I walk over and give my little sister a big hug. "Are you here alone? Or did Mom and Dad come with you?"

"Nope, just me. Sometimes I like to get you when you are alone. Otherwise, I feel like I have to fight to get a moment alone with you."

"Do you want some lemonade?"

"Sure, I'll go grab a glass. Meet ya on the porch, or do you want to sit outside?"

"How about we stay out here? That way, if anyone comes home or arrives early, we'll have a bit more time before they find us. I'll go in with you and refill my glass. Then we can sit on the back patio."

I'm sensing that my little sister is either nervous or upset about something. Hopefully, I can get it out of her before everyone else shows up, and she clams back up without spilling what's on her mind.

"Stella, spill. You're off, and I want to know what is going on with you. Are you okay?"

"Jules, I'm good. Yesterday, at the farmers market, I met this woman. She is thinking of opening a store on the square and asked me if I would be open to talking to her about being one of her vendors. She is opening a wellness type of store but is also hoping to carry local business products."

"Stella! That sounds amazing. You know I'm your biggest supporter of your bath salts. What is the part you are struggling with?"

"It's just a lot of pressure, and what if I can't keep up with how much she wants, or what if I make something that someone doesn't like? What if I fail?"

"Ah, but what if you don't fail? What if you don't take a chance and miss out on an amazing opportunity? I believe in you, sweetie, and if I have learned anything these last couple of months, it's that you must believe in yourself. I believe in you, and so does everyone that loves you."

"So, you think I should do it?"

"Absolutely! We can talk about it more over coffee with the girls if you want. They may have some advice to offer that I don't. Why don't you just start with a few staple things and see how it goes. Start with just a handful of scents but with the whole line: salts, soaps, lotions. See how that goes, and then maybe add new scents?"

"I am SO glad I came to you, Jules. I think that helps me wrap my head around it, so thanks."

She wraps her arms around me and gives me a huge bear hug. I just smile, knowing that she will be fine. Maybe we both will take our new opportunities and soar. We relax a little longer before everyone starts arriving for dinner and planning.

The doorbell rings, and I walk to open it. I see Griffin and Hillary getting out of the catering van. *Why the hell are they driving that here today?*
Griffin starts waving, "Hey, sweets, can you send out a couple of your hunky brothers or Jacks?"

"Sure, hold on-wait, why? What the heck did you bring

you guys?"

"Come on, darling...send the hunky boys, please. Explain later."

I go back into the house and ask Jackson and Rob to go out and help Griffin with whatever the heck he needs. Most likely, he just wants to watch them move around and get in his fill. Laughing, I walk back into the house and join the rest who are here already. They can humor Griffin and do whatever he has up his sleeve.

"Stella, your bestie is in front, ogling the guys, so you may need to rescue him if he gets too handsy with Rob."

"On it." She jumps up and heads out front.

Sitting there with Mom and Dad and Jackson's parents, I start to hear a lot of commotion from the front. I hear Hillary and Garrett in a heated discussion and then Jackson cutting it off. I get up and head towards them.

"What's going on.... why do you have your enormous whiteboard from your shop with you, Hill?"

Garrett says, "See-as usual, you went overboard!"

If lightning could strike from a stare, Hillary would have just torched my brother. "You see, GARRETT, Jules asked us here to PLAN and HELP her. I came prepared so all our ideas can be written on the whiteboard. So, just suck it!"

"Settle down, Garrett. Hillary, thank you! This is a great idea, although I am sure it wasn't easy getting that over here. But it'll be great to have it and see all our ideas."

Griff says with a snicker, "Oh, it wasn't HARD to get that thing in here. The boys did a great job lifting and carrying that in here." Clapping his hands with a mischievous smile, he says, "Well done, boys, well done."

Laughing, Jackson grabs Griffin. "Come on, Griff, before you get yourself in trouble, let's grab you a beer."

"Oh, honey, that sounds lovely."

Chapter Thirty-Two

Jackson

After everyone has arrived and we've all eaten our BBQ and dessert, I stand up and get everyone's attention. Julia and I kept brushing off questions since their arrival, so I guess it's time to let the cat out of the bag.

"Jules, come here, sweetheart. You need to be here with me to make your announcement." I watch my wife make her way over to me and everyone is quiet, wondering what we have to say.

"First of all, Jules and I want to thank you all for being here with us today, and most importantly, for your love and support. We may not have made it to this point without your assistance in our Five Dates, and it sure wouldn't have been as much of an adventure. The reason for today is to let you in on a little secret and then to help us navigate our next steps. But I think my beautiful wife here needs to be the one to share the announcement with you. Jules?"

Smiling, she leans into me, gives me a kiss, and then looks at all of our friends and family, "Okay, I know you're all dying to know why we've brought you here today. Jackson secretly bought me the Yellow Lady because we had always dreamed of living there and raising our family. Since we both love our current home and don't want to move, we're going to use the Yellow Lady for something else. I've decided to start my own business using the Yellow Lady, changing her name to Harte of Harmony, and turning her into an intimate event space and bed and breakfast. We asked all of you here to help me brainstorm how to make that happen. So, what do you all say? Care to help us?"

At once, everyone started congratulating us on being the proud new owners and were very excited to hear what Jules wants to do with the space. I see my parents looking at me, and they slowly walk over together.

"Jackson, that is quite the announcement. It looks like things between the two of you are on stronger ground again. It's obvious that you've made your wife very happy. How are things going on your side of things, though? Have you made any headway for changes at the office?"

"Yes, I have and thank you for bringing that up. That is part two of our announcement. Jules, can you come back over here a minute?"

Julia walks back over to me and says, "Okay, everyone-we are going to get to brainstorming in a second, but we have one more announcement to make tonight." She squeezes my hand and gives me a wink. "Go ahead, Jackson."

"Most of you know that I've been swamped at work. That was the real reason behind my family being off these last couple of months. Jules has been working on finding her balance and realizing what she needs. While she was working on her side of things, I was doing my own fair share of personal reflection and trying to find a way to have a better work-life balance. I'm happy to announce that my friend, Dr. Noah Roarke, will become a partner at my practice in the next couple of months. He's currently working in Chicago but wants a change, too, so he has agreed to become my partner. That will help me not miss so much with all of you. I've realized that with all the growth that Lake Harmony is having, it meant my practice was growing just as quickly, and it wasn't something I could keep up with anymore. I just didn't realize it quickly enough, so it took Jules hitting me over the head to see I needed to make changes, too. So, thank you again for supporting our family and always making sure we were on the right path. We couldn't do all this without you guys."

∞ ∞ ∞

We spend a couple more hours brainstorming all the things that need to be done, and everyone asking to be assigned to jobs. Sam and Paul agreed to help Jules work in the gardens since that is their area of expertise. Since they always have teenagers and retired veterans that want to work with them, they figured we would be able to get some help with cleaning up around the house and getting the flower beds back to their full potential.

The guys all volunteered to build a gazebo near the gardens to make another area that could be used as an outdoor altar for weddings or special moments. They're also going to oversee creating a parking area and walkways to the house that won't interfere with the view but are accessible from the long drive.

Dad is going to tackle refinishing all the floors and opening the two rooms. He said his crew would handle that, and he gave us some great ideas to make a folding partition so that Julia could use the space as one or two rooms, depending on the need. Rob is going to oversee updating the kitchen, and Hillary will help with the layout and appliances, so it is the best setup for large events and preparing food.

Both moms are excited to help but want to focus on creating the interior spaces with the furnishings and décor. While brainstorming, we decided that the guest suites upstairs would all be named after flowers: Daisy, Jasmine, Lily, Rose, and Sunflower, with coordinating colors and accessories.

The girls all volunteered to help with preparing all the marketing for the new business and figuring out how to advertise and create a website with pictures of each area. Everyone laughed and said this is the perfect opportunity to bring Gertie and Harmony Hears into the mix. She can put posts up for us and get the word out. Everyone reads that Facebook page whether they admit it or not. Speaking of Gertie, we should get the ball rolling with an update for her. I may pop in there tomorrow on my way to work and give her a little update.

Epilogue

Julia

Two months later

All the remodeling and updates are done. The final inspection passed, and we are all set to go. I think this is a great time to have everyone back out to toast before the grand opening. Grabbing my phone, I send out a group text.

Julia: Who's ready to celebrate?
Julia: We passed the final inspection and can open!!!
Julia: When/Where: Next Saturday @ 7:30pm, Harte of Harmony
Julia: Champagne on the house *Wink emoji*
Jackson: SO proud of you honey
Rob: Food?
Garrett: Bring chips Rob LOL
Rob: Cool-done
Hillary: I will provide apps to serve
Bree: Bringing surprise
Julia: Do tell
Bree: Surprise Jules
Sam: Paul and I will be there with??? LMK
Cooper: Will drop by but then gotta get back to bar (Saturday)
Dad Harte: Mom and I wouldn't miss it
Mom: Dad and I are so proud of you!!!!
Stella: YAY *heart emoji*
Ellen: Need help setting up? Scott and I can come early *Smiley emoji*
Griffin: Yay, booze and boys!
Julia: Griff -LOL, behave
Rob: Is this like Date 58542?
Jackson: Very funny wise guy

Good! All set. One more invite I want to make sure goes out. I call his number and he answers, "Hello, Dr. Roarke speaking."

"Noah, it's Julia. What are you doing this Saturday evening?"

∞∞∞∞

After stopping for fresh flowers and giving Gertie the scoop, she posted a lovely announcement on Facebook in Harmony Hears.

Harte Of Harmony Grand Opening (Fka The Yellow Lady)
Our own Julia Harte has put her heart and soul into rehabbing our majestic lady on the bluff and turning her into a beautiful, new intimate venue. Do you have a special occasion coming up and need a place to host your family and friends? Do you want to have a special occasion and privacy? Do you need a quiet and private space to hold a meeting? If you said YES to any of these things, then GO SEE Julia @ Harte of Harmony. Hurry and schedule with her now before all of Chicagoland discovers the beautiful and magical location she has created.

I have fresh flowers in all the guest suites upstairs and around the house downstairs. I put a long table down the center of the large open event space where Hillary can put all the appetizers. I opened the beautiful partition doors that Dad made for the room. I already set up the champagne bar with beer and wine. The lights are on and now all I need are my guests to arrive.

"Honey, everything looks amazing. I just walked through all the bedroom suites, and I love what our moms have done. I like that you added a plaque to each door with the flower, so guests know which room they have. Stella did an amazing job putting her salts, soaps, and lotions in each bath. I love that she can be part of this with you. Is this anything else I can do for you?"

"Yep, I need a kiss from my handsome husband. Think

200

you can give me that?"

Grabbing me around the waist and pulling me in tight into his chest, he looks at me, and his thumb goes to the corner of my lip. "I am so in love with you, Jules. You've made this house into an amazing place that everyone is going to come to and fall in love with just like we did over 20 years ago. I am so proud of you."

He leans in, and his kiss goes from soft and loving to something more desperate and intimate in a heartbeat. I think I hear someone clearing their throat, and then I hear Griffin shout, "Getting sexy with Jackson! Yes! Sorry to interrupt."
Pulling back and laughing, I reply, "Whoops, sorry. Forgot where I was for a moment."

Griffin says, "No worries, please continue."

I step out of Jackson's arms, and with a wink I whisper to Griffin. "Oh, I will, but later and in private."

"You go, girl. Get you some of that sexy man later. I came to help Hill bring in all the apps, but that scene was way better than anything I expected. God, you two love birds make me miss sexy times. Well, shit, better go find Hill before she starts shrieking."

We watch Griffin go back out, and, slowly, one by one, everyone starts to show up. I tell everyone to please go ahead and wander through the house. Many of them haven't been here since we cleaned the house and added furniture and accessories. It will be fun to watch them walk through and see how it has all turned out.

I watch Bree come into the house and look for me. When she spots me, she smiles and heads my way.

"Oh my god, Jules, this place looks magical."

"Thank you, that's what I hoped everyone would think! I want to make it as magical to everyone as it's always been to Jackson and me."

"I can't wait to walk through and see what you did with the guest suites. I brought you something. I was in the city last week, and when I was in a cute little shop, I saw this and knew you needed to have it. Please open."

She hands me a beautifully wrapped square gift. It's so pretty! I almost hate to open it.

"Come on, you need to open it so we can memorialize this night."

I open the gift and see a beautiful guest book with an inscription inside the front cover-

Dearest Julia,

You only had to believe in yourself to make it happen. Congratulations on your Harte of Harmony—may it bring magic to all who walk through her doors. I am so proud of you for reaching for your dreams and pushing through any obstacles with grace and determination.

Love, Bree

Wiping a tear from my cheek, I grab Bree and give her a big hug. "Thank you, friend. I couldn't have done it without you, without all of you. I love you like a sister, Bree, and you just made my night."

"Love you too, Jules."

Standing there talking to Bree I look toward the front door and I see Noah walk in, look around, walk toward us and it seems he cannot take his eyes off Bree. Still only looking at Bree he says, "Hey, Julia, this place is gorgeous. I'm very impressed."

"Thank you, Noah. I'm so glad you could make it. I thought tonight would be a great time to meet some of our family and good friends. Now that you've moved into town and settled into the practice, we need to get you out and about a bit."

"Yeah, I'm finally unpacked and two weeks in with Jackson at the office, so things are beginning to feel a little more routine."

I am watching as Noah can't seem to take his eyes off Bree and she in turn is staring at him, but neither of them has even spoken to the other. This is interesting to watch and I couldn't be happier to see both of their reactions to each other.

"Noah, I'd like you to meet one of my best friends. This is Bree. We've been best friends since our childhood."

I watch as Noah takes Bree's hand and shakes it slowly looks at only her. "It's very nice to meet you, Bree. You know I work with Jackson, but what is it you do?"

I watch Bree still looking a bit frazzled, and answer for her. "Bree is a Kindergarten teacher here in Lake Harmony."Sorry, yes, I've been teaching kindergarten here since college. Growing up, I figured I would go away to college and not come back, but slowly we all do return. It's a great community to raise kids, and I have many friends here. So, I came back, and I've been teaching here since."

I don't think she took one breath throughout that entire explanation. Hmm, standing here with these two, I'm beginning to feel like a third wheel, "Sorry to leave you two, but Jackson is over there trying to get my attention. Bree, why don't you take Noah around and show him what we've done here for Harte of Harmony. You know your way around. Noah, I am so glad you could make it tonight. Make sure you grab a drink and some food after Bree shows you around."

I walk over to my husband and give him a kiss. "Thanks for the interruption—it was perfect timing, honey."

"Why, what's up? Your smile makes me believe you are up to something. I see Noah has arrived."

With a big smile, I look at my husband. "Yes, and it was fate because I was standing there with Bree."

"And?"

"And the sparks were so hot I was afraid I would catch fire."

"Oh, look at that Jules." We watch as Noah escorts Bree out of the room and up the stairs to look around the house.

"Isn't that interesting. How many dates do you think it will take them to realize they are perfect for each other?"

The End

Dear Reader,

This is the end of Julia and Jackson's story. Bree and Noah's story **Sexy Secrets**, *the second book in The Lake Harmony Series, will be available October 2022.*

About The Author

Tanja Waltrip

was born and raised in the 'burbs of Chicago and now resides in sunny Florida. She has a daughter, Emily, who lives in the Maryland/D.C. area. Despite the tumultuous nature of chasing the sun, one thing has remained the same—her voracious reading habit. She always knew that she would one day turn this passion for the Contemporary Romance genre into her own writing pursuit.

Please sign up for my NEWSLETTER to receive news about upcoming releases and giveaways at Tanjawaltrip.com

Made in United States
Orlando, FL
20 July 2022